MY LIFE
WITH LUKAS

(On Topanga Canyon Boulevard)

TAILSPIN

ERIC A. WALTERS

Edited by Katie Naum

WHERE THERE'S A WILL.
THERE'S A WAY.

Under One Roof

Under each roof in the city
There's a house, a home, a story
(Our own story)
Open up your eyes
There's a big surprise

And it's right there where you live.
There's someone to trust a secret
Maybe the father that you dreamed of
The guy who won't talk smack
The son that you never had
You got all your best friends
Right here under one roof.

Unter Uns Theme (Modified)

PROLOGUE

I am Noah Whitmore, thirty-five-year old physics teacher from Topanga, California. Until a year ago, my career was my life and my life was my career. Some argued that I had no personal life at all. They would be right. I have been described as conformist, introverted, organized, meticulous and highly sarcastic. I would drive the same route to and from school every day; order the same meal at my favorite restaurant; and plan my curriculum weeks, if not months, in advance. I was a creature of habit; I liked regularity and order in my life.

My life was irrevocably changed when my teenage cousin Lukas arrived in Topanga. My cousin Lisa was his mother; when she and her husband were faced with the intersection of professional careers and being "present" parents, their professional careers won out. As always, I "did the right thing" and offered to take Lukas in for a few months. Little did I know that, as time passed, the probably of Lukas remaining in Topanga permanently increased as well.

Lukas is a talented soccer player and a bit of a troublemaker. The "misunderstood teen" with a heart of gold, Lukas could easily go with the flow. He struggled to succeed academically in school and was often in the principal's office for some little stunt he pulled. With his brown curly hair and gangly body, he was often mistaken for the actor Timothée Chalamet.

Tailspin picks up where Best Kid Ever leaves off, when Lukas and I learned that his mother had been killed in a drunk driving accident.

Fortunately, his time in Topanga had given Lukas the guidance and structure he so desperately needed and had given me an escape from a solitary, regimented existence.

I found a family with Lukas on Topanga Canyon Boulevard.

Lukas found a new family with me on Topanga Canyon Boulevard.

And so continues the story of my life with Lukas. On Topanga Canyon Boulevard.

ONE

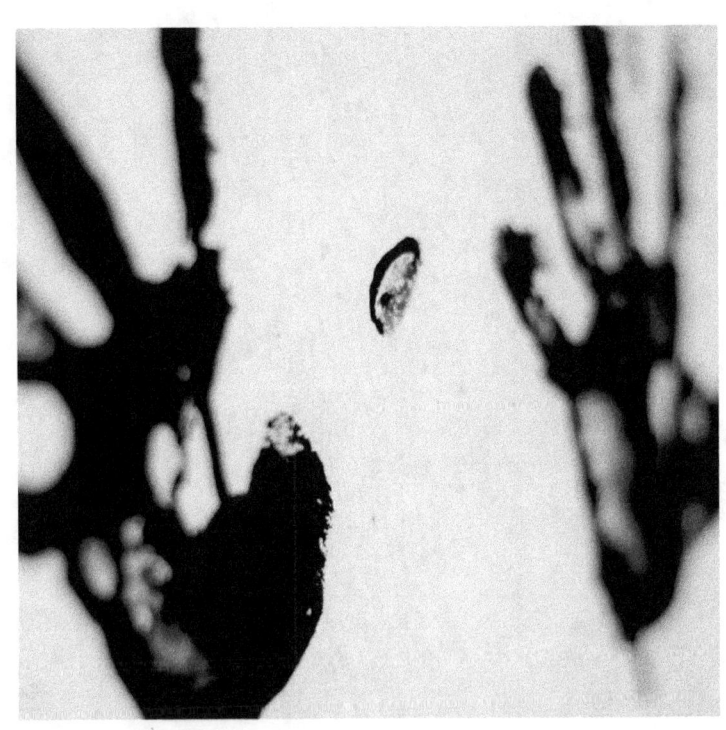

When his mother Lisa was killed by a drunk driver in Miami, my cousin Lukas and I were overwhelmed. He was devastated and regretted not talking with her when he had the chance. And even though Lisa and I, as first cousins, had drifted apart somewhat over the past few years, I was equally as devastated. After all, she had entrusted me with the care of her son. Attending her funeral would be a challenge for me—and an even greater challenge for Lukas.

Lukas had faced numerous challenges over the past five months since he moved across country to live with me in Topanga. He'd slowly acclimated to a new way of life in southern California, growing to accept living with a square high school physics teacher. I'd grown to accept that I was responsible for a goofy, yet charming, soccer-playing teenager. We'd both grown to respect each other more than we might publicly admit.

Lisa's professional family—the television news community—mourned the loss of a trusted journalist and talented colleague. Tributes had been pouring in all day: the church was filled with floral arrangements from across the planet, and the funeral home's website had been flooded with remembrances, tributes, and condolences. Lisa was both well-loved and respected.

Lukas sat quietly in the front pew, nervously tapping his left foot. He looked around and could not identify any of the hundreds of people in the church. He knew me, his dad, and his best buddy Max, but that was it.

"Who are all these people?" Lukas asked me. He held onto my hand so tightly I thought he was going to break it.

Rev. Williams began his eulogy. His words sounded like they had been co-opted from Lisa's *New York Times* obituary. It was clear that he barely knew Lisa at all.

I thought back to my own mother's funeral. My mother was a well-loved and well-respected teacher at Encino High, who had also died at the hands of a drunk driver when I was a freshman in high school. I remembered sitting in the church at her funeral; there wasn't an empty seat or dry eye in the house. As a teacher, my mother had touched the lives of countless aspiring scientists. It was then that I decided that I wanted to become a teacher as well.

After the eulogy, Lisa's husband Peter spoke briefly. He had remained stoic ever since the accident, and shared very few words. Then Rev. Williams called Lukas up to the ambo.

"I don't think I can do this," Lukas whispered. He squeezed my hand even harder. I reminded him of what I had said just before the funeral began. "You're Lukas Whitmore. You can do this."

As Lukas stood up and walked to the front, I looked down. He had worn his black Converse sneakers with his Hugo Boss suit. It was such a Lukas look. I'd bet even his look-alike Timothée Chalamet would be impressed.

Lukas stood at the ambo and looked down at the Bible before looking out over the congregation. He wiped a tear from his eye, looked down at me, and smiled. He then stared at the casket for a minute before pushing his curly hair out of his face.

"I don't see a lot of familiar faces here today," he finally said. "I guess my mom was respected by a lot of people. The faces I do recognize me a lot to me. I'm going to keep it simple. Mom, I love you. You've left me in good hands."

Lukas left the altar, slowly walking over to his mother's casket and kissing it before returning to his seat. His dad made an effort to hug him, but Lukas turned and gave me a hug instead. Peter mumbled something I could not hear.

Lukas whispered to me, "You're the only adult here that cares for me." I didn't know whether to feel happy or sad. I had to believe, though, that deep down, Peter cared for Lukas as well.

The service soon ended. Lisa had opted for a private burial, and Lukas graciously thanked every mourner as they headed out. As the last person left the church, he shook out his hand.

The service at the cemetery was equally short. The minister blessed the casket. Peter slowly approached the casket, wiping a tear from his eye. Peter was often stoic; I had rarely seen him show any emotions. He stood over the casket for several minutes. When Peter turned around, the redness of his face along with the moisture around his eyes suggested he'd been more emotionally impacted than he would have publicly let on.

He motioned for Lukas to stand next to him. Lukas remained next to me and grasped my hand again tightly.

"You should go stand next to your dad," I told Lukas.

"Why should I? He's barely stood next to me my whole life," Lukas replied bluntly.

"You'll regret this moment if you don't," I whispered back to him.

Lukas released my hand, and fortunately, my blood started to flow again. I felt feeling slowly creep back in my hand as I watched Lukas stand next to his dad for a minute or two. Peter tried to give Lukas a hug again, and Lukas turned away from him once more. It was a cold moment. I envisioned Lukas, many years in the future, appearing on Dr. Phil, describing his unresolved issues with his father.

Lukas returned to my side after just a few moments. He started crying and grasped my hand again.

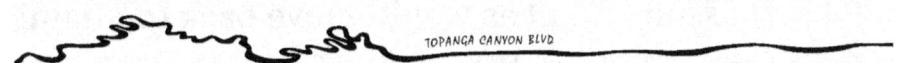

When we returned to the house, it took only a few seconds for Lukas to change out of the Hugo Boss suit and into a pair of shorts and a T-shirt. He lay down out by the pool and quickly fell asleep. This would have been a hard day for anyone, but he had managed to keep his composure throughout the funeral, the receiving line and the private burial. Part of me believed he wasn't quite ready to talk about his mother's death. After living with Lukas for the past six months, I'd learned he would only share his feelings when he was ready to, not when he was forced to.

I sat in the living room, nursing a cup of coffee. I remembered being overtired and overwhelmed myself, after my own mother's funeral. I was ready to fall asleep too, when Peter unexpectedly walked in through the unlocked door.

He sat down on the chair next to me and spoke without any greeting. "We need to talk about Lukas," he said.

"What about him?"

"I think he needs to stay with you throughout the summer," Peter continued.

I had assumed Lukas would move back to Miami permanently, but in the back of my mind I was considering his request to stay in Topanga for the summer. Still, I didn't want to be presumptive. "He just lost his mom. You just lost your wife," I said. "Don't you think you should be together as a family unit?"

Peter explained that he was contemplating selling the house in Miami and moving to Paris full time for work. I was floored. "Would you bring Lukas with you?" I asked.

"I'm not sure he'd be too keen on moving," Peter said. "Especially after the way he behaved today."

I immediately felt defensive on Lukas' behalf, whom I thought had behaved very well under very trying circumstances. "Do you blame him?" I asked. "Six months ago, you sent him packing because you didn't want to deal with him. Now you want to do the same thing again."

As I spoke, I looked up to see Lukas standing at the patio door. He was in my line of sight but behind his dad.

"He knows I care," Peter said. Lukas rolled his eyes.

I usually kept my temper, but now my anger started boiling over. "I don't think he does. And you know how I know? I don't think he's mentioned you once in the last six months. And did you see who he stood next to today—me, not you. I've been more a dad to him in California than you have your whole life."

Peter stiffened up in his chair and his face turned red. "How dare you?" he demanded. "Don't forget you're in my house. I didn't have you here to insult me."

I looked past Peter to Lukas. He was shocked, but then a huge smile came over his face as our eyes met.

Meanwhile Peter unleashed what must have been years of perceived failure as a dad on me. "Just because you've never had kids—and probably never will—doesn't mean you can steal mine," he said.

That hurt very deeply. My friends and colleagues knew I struggled with relationships. Perhaps it was the death of my mother that drove me to shy away from finding someone special. Maybe deep down, I was afraid to commit to a meaningful relationship. Maybe deep down, I was afraid I would just end up losing that person. Just like Lukas, I was often reticent to share my feelings, and as my life and my career had progressed, I found myself committing more and more time to my teaching. Lukas' arrival last winter had slowly changed that pattern, making me more willing to put work aside to be there for him.

I glared at Peter. "I'm not trying to steal your son. Lisa was the one who came to me for help. Lisa was the one that asked me to look after Lukas. I was more than happy to do it." I looked back over at Lukas after I said that, and he smiled and gave me two thumbs up. My stock was rising with him at least.

Peter relaxed a little. "I'm sorry. I know it's been a stressful situation for all of us." He sighed irritably. "I'm not sure what to do," he admitted.

I realized that having an emotional battle with Peter wasn't going to help—he was clearly struggling with making the right decision for his son. I knew I needed to take the high road and make a grand gesture.

"I'm sorry for being rude," I began. "You know, Lukas has just a few weeks left in the semester. He also asked to stay through the summer, and you clearly have a lot on your plate. I'm happy to have him for the summer. That will give you time to figure out what might be the best path going forward."

This satisfied Peter at last, and he reached out and shook my hand. I looked past him again at Lukas standing at the patio door. He was crying now.

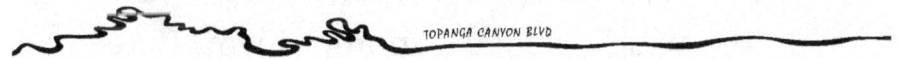
TOPANGA CANYON BLVD

We settled into our bulkhead seats for our flight back from Miami to Los Angeles. Lukas slumped down in his seat and put his black Converse sneakers against the wall in front of him. The flight attendant glared at him, but as long as Lukas was comfortable, Lukas was happy.

"I can't believe you yelled at my dad," he said in awe.

I hadn't really yelled at Peter—maybe raised my voice. Yelling at people was not my style. "Maybe I was firm with him," I admitted.

Lukas had been even more firm with his dad. When Peter had offered his hand as a peace offering at the airport, Lukas had just looked at him and walked away. I don't think Lukas had really ever gotten over the comment that was made the January before: "Had we known how much trouble he would be, we might have reconsidered having a kid." The comment hurt back then and it still hurt today.

"Are you doing ok?" I asked. I was deeply concerned about his well-being.

Lukas said nothing for a while and just kept moving the window shade up and down. It seemed like he just wanted to annoy the flight attendant.

"I'm really tired of people asking me that," he finally admitted.

I remembered people asking me the same question after my mother's funeral. "I promise not to ask you that again," I said. Then I thought I'd try a different subject. "Did you say goodbye to Max?"

"I did. Although we'll still Snap a lot."

"You guys have been friends for a long time, right?" I asked.

Lukas stopped playing with the window shade. "We've been best buds ever since the first day of first grade," he said.

"Was he ok with you spending the summer in California?"

Lukas paused. He had never admitted that he missed his best friend during his entire time in Topanga. They were inseparable when Lukas lived in Florida.

"Like I said, we'll Snap a lot," he replied at last, but he sounded unsure of himself.

"Maybe you'd like to visit him over the summer? Or have him come out to California?" I asked. If Lukas needed me to pay for a ticket, I would.

"That's nice of you to offer! Actually, Max is spending the summer at a home stay in Germany."

"Maybe you'd like to try something like that, too?"

Lukas laughed at that idea. "I have trouble staying with one family. You want me to stay with another?" he joked.

"I was thinking it might help you with your college resume," I suggested. "And get you out to explore the world."

"Max is more of a college resume builder," Lukas sighed. "I don't even know if I'm good enough for college."

I knew Lukas was very bright—just not college-ready yet. "I think you're too young to know what you want to do for the rest of your life," I told him.

Lukas didn't reply, just put his headphones on and transitioned into his mellow mode, indicating that the conversation was over. Within a few minutes, he was fast asleep.

I looked over Lukas, contorted like a pretzel in his seat. For the first time in a long time, he looked peaceful. I could only hope that sense of peacefulness would last.

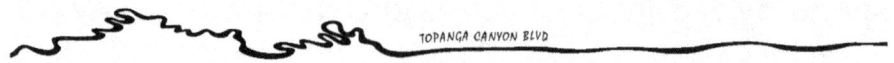
TOPANGA CANYON BLVD

We landed on time at LAX. Lukas had grown fidgety toward the end of the flight, and was anxious to get moving, but the passengers in first class were clearly not in a hurry. In spite of this, he waited patiently to deplane, and even thanked the flight attendant.

The baggage claim was busy for a late afternoon, and we struggled to make our way through the crowds to carousel number three. I spotted my dad Matt sitting in a chair by the door, sipping a cup of Dunkin' coffee. He waved when we saw us, and slowly got up and made his way over to us.

"How was the flight?" he asked.

"Uneventful. He slept through most of it," I replied, pointing to Lukas.

Lukas stretched his arms and let out a deep yawn. "Never enough sleep," he announced. He sat down on the edge of the baggage carousel, feeling the need to touch every bag that passed by from a previous flight.

"How's he doing?" my dad asked quietly. He was concerned about Lukas' well-being. There were times I'd wished he'd shown the same concern for me when I was growing up.

"He seems to be in pretty good spirits, considering." I remembered how I felt after my mother died. "He's just tired of people asking him how he is doing." I couldn't blame him for that.

The alarm went off, indicating that the luggage from our flight was approaching the baggage carousel. Lukas bounced to his feet and yelled, "Here comes the luggage!" The other travelers gave him an odd look.

I pulled Lukas back from the edge of the carousel and told the elderly couple standing next to him, "Don't mind him. He has problems," I said sarcastically.

Lukas looked agitated. "Dude, I don't have problems. I'm just complex."

Just then, my dad called out my name and told us to turn around. He quickly snapped a picture of Lukas and me.

"Welcome back to California. And welcome home," he said.

TWO

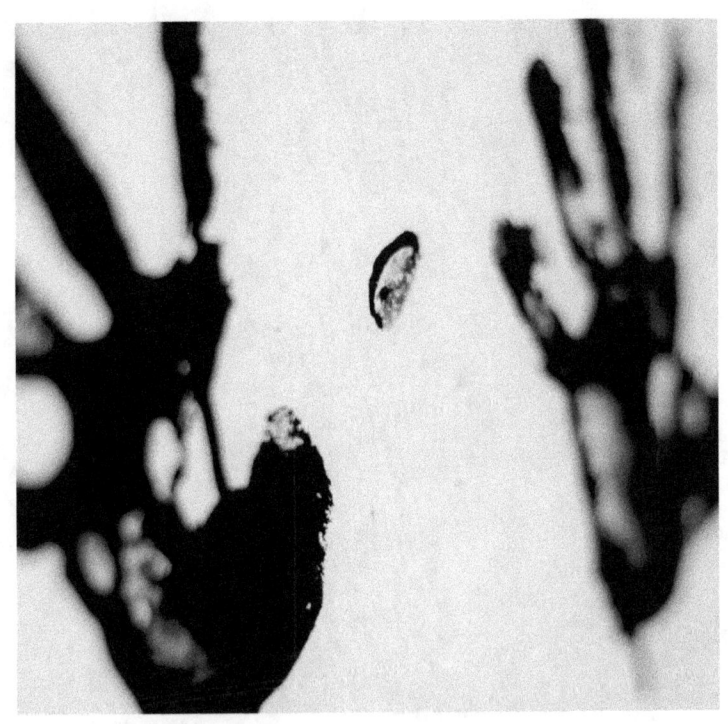

I woke up early on Saturday morning, the next day, ready to head to Ralph's by 7 AM for my regular weekly grocery shopping. Peeking into Lukas' room, I saw him sound asleep in the fetal position, completely entangled in his blanket. I was tempted to wake him and encourage him to get started on the schoolwork he had missed the previous week. But I knew "Saturday morning" and "schoolwork" were two phrases Lukas never used the same sentence. Lukas liked sleeping in on Saturday unless he had a soccer game. He needed his beauty sleep.

I moved through the aisles of Ralph's, where my cart filled up quickly. Ever since Lukas had joined me, not only had the number of shopping bags I took home quadrupled, my weekly food budget had quadrupled as well. Lukas could eat 5000 calories a day and still remain thin as a rail. I wasn't sure if genetics, athletics, or burning off nervous energy kept the weight off him. Meanwhile, I could eat one cookie and feel my blood sugar shoot up instantly. It was a curse being diabetic.

I was struggling to push my full shopping cart out to my car when I heard someone call out, "You're back, I see!" Turning, I saw my colleague Pat approach me. Her empty cart moved easily under her gentle push.

I told Pat that we'd gotten back the afternoon before. She glanced over my cart. "Lukas must be back with you. You'd never need that much food for yourself."

"Yes," I replied, "he's going to finish up the school year here and then stay through the summer while his dad sorts out what he wants to do."

Pat seemed surprised. "He needs time to figure out what to do? It seems like that would be an easy decision for any father."

"Peter might move to Paris. Leaving Lukas behind," I admitted. I hated even saying it. *How could a father just abandon his son like that?* I thought.

Pat tactfully changed the subject. "Why don't you and Lukas and I meet me for some breakfast at Malibu Coffee and Tea once he's up?" she asked. "It'll be great to see him again and catch up." I agreed.

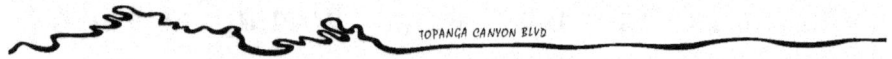

TOPANGA CANYON BLVD

Lukas was jolted awake by a nightmare, his Chalamet hair matted in sweat against his forehead. He couldn't remember the dream exactly, but he was pretty sure it involved him standing alone on the beach with his father walking away from him. Even at his age, bad dreams still scared him. He liked happy dreams about happy people in happy places.

As Lukas pulled a fresh pair of khaki shorts and a T shirt out of his dresser, he felt another pang of shock as his eyes took in a picture of him and his mother that was stuck to the side of the drawer. Lukas and Lisa were standing in front of their family Christmas tree. The photo had been taken just before he had moved to California. The world had changed so much for him since then.

He stared at the photo for a while, then gently traced a finger over the image of his mother. It still hurt him that he had not called her back the night she died; he fought back a tear as he wrestled with this feeling. Other images swam through his mind.

Lukas and his mom at his elementary school graduation.

Lukas and his mom building sand castles at the beach.

Lukas and his mom at the middle school athletic awards.

Lukas being named Middle School soccer MVP.

So many good memories. He kissed the photo of his mom and then slid it into the Bible he had stuffed at the back of his drawer.

After dressing, Lukas quickly scrawled a note and stuck it on his mirror before heading out the door.

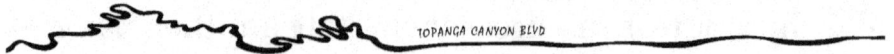

As I opened the front door, I yelled to Lukas to come help me unload the groceries from the car. The house was silent. I assumed Lukas was still fast asleep in his bed.

I peeked into his room again. His bed was an empty tangle of sheets. Heaven forbid he would actually make his bed! Looking around the room, I noticed a note stuck to his mirror. It simply stated, "I just need some time alone."

I had a pretty good idea of where he had gone, and decided to give him the time and space he needed. As I left his room, I saw the two blue handprints on the back of his door, and smiled. How the world had changed for me since then.

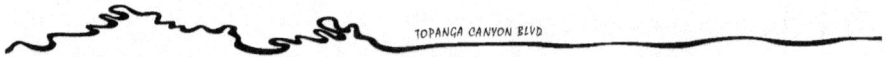

Lukas was dripping in sweat by the time he arrived at the Top of the Topanga. He'd skateboarded, then walked, then skateboarded again the ten-mile distance from our house on Emmerdale Trail. I always thought he was nuts for traveling this far this way, but he had explained before that the solitude on the skateboard and the solitude at the overlook gave him time to just reflect, think or be alone. One time I offered to accompany him, but I was told that the Top of Topanga was his space. I wanted to respect that.

Lukas sprawled out on his favorite bench, the one that overlooked Woodland Hills below. If he looked hard enough, he could see Ventura Boulevard as well as Westfield Topanga. He'd grabbed a bagel on the way out the door, but even so, he had a hankering for a kabob from Masses Kabobery. He stretched his legs out, amazed that after all this time in California, they were still white. His legs never tanned. They just burned to a lobster red.

He wiped the sweat from his forehead and put his grey beanie on to cover his sweaty, unkempt hair. The overlook was quiet now, but in a few hours, as noon approached, it would be teeming with amateur photographers and birders.

He heard the gravel behind him crunch. Turning around, he saw a black Mercedes pull up toward him. His friend Emery got out of the car, and Lukas stood up to greet his best buddy.

Emery grabbed Lukas in a bear hug and gave him a pat on the back. "Man, I've missed you," he said.

"Dude, I've missed you too. But please don't ask me how I'm doing."

Emery could be as much of a wiseass as Lukas. "So, how are you doing?" he deadpanned.

Lukas whacked him in the arm. "Jerk."

Emery grew more serious. "No, seriously. How was the funeral? We were all worried about you."

"No one should ever have to go through that." Lukas sighed irritably as he relived the experience. "The church was packed. Packed with *reporters*. Very few friends."

Emery smirked. "That's what happens when you spend your life doing work."

Lukas laughed. "Don't look at me. I've spent my life avoiding work!"

The two of them sat down on the bench. "Do you need to talk?" Emery asked. "Or—do you want to talk?"

Lukas laughed again. "It's funny—everyone keeps asking me that too."

Emery paused respectfully. "I can let you just sit here."

Lukas felt relieved. He always felt safe around Emery. "I found an old pic of my mom and me in my dresser drawer this morning," he said, opening up. "A lot of good memories came flooding back. And then I realized I don't have any pictures of my dad and me." He paused. "I guess that doesn't bother me."

"Considering how you parted ways before you got here, it doesn't surprise me."

"I don't know," Lukas hedged. "I might have been a little rude to him at the funeral."

"Funerals are very emotional. I'm sure he knows you really didn't mean it." Emery always looked for the best in every situation.

Lukas hesitated a moment before speaking again. "You know what I asked Noah just before my mom died?"

"I think you told me, but I forgot."

"I asked him if I could stay for the summer."

Emery looked surprised. "You must really like it out here."

"I like it because it's not *there*. It's not Miami. I liked it that way even before my mom died. But now—I just don't see anything to pull me back to Miami."

"What about Max?"

Lukas smiled. "Max will always be one of my best friends, no matter where we are."

"Are you staying?" Emery asked.

The answer was yes. Lukas assured Emery that they too would be best friends, no matter where they were.

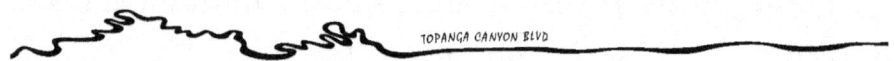

I pulled into the parking lot of Malibu Coffee + Tea. As usual for a Saturday morning, the parking lot was busy and the line was long—but moving quickly. I spotted Pat's bike locked in the bike rack. If she could cycle everywhere, she would. If she could run everywhere, she would. That explained her very toned calves. Mine, on the other hand, could use a trip or two or three to the gym.

I grabbed my midnight mocha iced coffee and found Pat sitting alone at a table on the deck. I slid into the chair opposite her and took a deep breath of the fresh Pacific Ocean air. No June gloom this morning, just sunny skies for miles.

We sat silently for a moment together, before hearing giggling behind us. Three of my physics students—Pietra, Rebecca, and Mikaela—were sitting at the next table.

"Hi Mr. Whitmore! Hi Dr. Branigan!" they proclaimed in unison, waving. I'd been a teacher long enough to understand how excited students got when they saw their teacher at the mall or at the supermarket. Students always seemed to pop up in the most unexpected places, so I always made sure I looked presentable when out in public.

We smiled and waved back at them, respectfully giving them space—we'd both paid full attention during the "boundaries" workshop the school organized. I knew the girls each had a major crush on Lukas, and now I was sure they thought Pat and I were dating. Pietra, Rebecca, and Mikaela finished their breakfast a few moments later and got up to leave.

"See you Monday," Pietra called out.

"See you on Monday, ladies. Make sure you have that problem set finished!" I reminded them.

"Make sure you say hi to Lukas. Tell him we are sorry about his mom," Rebecca added earnestly.

It's one of the things I loved most about teaching. No matter how challenging it could be working with teenagers, I really felt that my students cared about their teachers, their education, and each other. Being a teacher was the best job on the planet.

The giggle-fest restarted as the trio headed out to the parking lot. Our "morning coffee date" would be front page news at Malibu High on Monday—unless the trio had moved on to some new piece of gossip by then.

Pat turned the conversation to a more important matter. "Where's Lukas?" she asked. I explained that he needed some alone time. He was out of the house when I'd returned from Ralph's.

"How's he holding up?" she continued. She had put her psychologist hat on.

"As well as can be expected." I couldn't help but laugh a little. "I think he's getting tired of people asking him how he's holding up."

"And how was the funeral?" she said, taking this in stride.

"As well as could be expected. Lukas was a trooper."

"And how are *you* holding up?"

Pat was always good about being a psychologist even when you were never quite sure you needed one. She knew Lisa and I were very close, and that her sudden death rocked me to the core. Pat also knew that I rarely shared my emotions and feelings with anyone. The last week would have been draining even for a person without any obligations. Having Lukas to worry about was an additional responsibility, one I wasn't sure I handled correctly. There was a lot going on inside that I hadn't dealt with yet.

"I'm doing ok," I said finally. "Just tired."

"Seriously? You just lost a close friend and family member." Pat also knew how and when to probe for additional information.

"I'll be able to handle it," I said.

"Handle it how?" she asked.

I always struggled to handle my own emotions, even privately. I had not been too successful in that endeavor so far—even after my own mother's death. Especially after my own mother's death. To this day, I don't think I've really gotten over it—or talked about it.

I sought to deflect the attention away from me. "I'm more worried about dealing with Lukas going forward."

"Why's that?" Pat asked, continue to probe.

I told her that I was ok with Lukas staying with me for the spring semester. We'd managed to build a rather solid pseudo-dad/pseudo-son relationship over the past few months, and I'd come to value his presence in my life. Still, I wasn't sure I could handle that responsibility for an extended period of time.

"You don't think there's a reason Lukas ended up out here with you?" Pat replied. She always asked incisive questions.

I knew the discussion she wanted to have. I decided to preempt it.

"I know what you're going to say. I can't work all the time. I need someone to care for in my life. You've said it before. You'll say it again." The words came out slowly, reluctantly. I struggled to admit these things to her—or even to myself.

"I've known you for ten years," Pat began. "You told me once that, ever since your mother died, you've been determined to carry on her legacy. To make a difference in the lives of your students, the same way your mother did. The same way your mother was making a difference in that one student's life the night she was killed."

I had to admit, her analysis was on point. Still, my whole body tightened up as I took in these words. Even twenty years later, I didn't like talking about my mother's death. I just wanted my students to find success, in whatever field they pursued—the same thing my mother wanted for her students. Something told me my mother was still looking down over the young woman she was trying to help the night she was killed. That student had become a successful Hollywood lawyer.

I wanted success in my own field, as well—with whatever sacrifices I needed to make. I knew my mother was looking down on me, too—just as I knew Lisa was looking down on Lukas.

Pat watched as I sat silently taking her words in. "Don't you think Lukas has given you a little bit more freedom?" she observed.

"Don't you think Lukas has given me one more person to take care of?" I countered.

"He's family—that's different. Don't you think you're playing the role you wish your mom had been able to continue to play for you?"

"I can't argue with that," I admitted. Having Lukas here didn't necessarily get me out of the house more, but I did find myself a little more relaxed, and a little more willing to let schoolwork go until the next day. I deeply appreciated the subtle changes in my life that Lukas had brought about. Even more importantly, I finally had a kid of my own—so to speak—to talk about at the faculty lunch table!

"So, what's the plan going forward?" Pat shifted back to her role as a supportive friend and colleague.

I told her that Lukas' dad and I had agreed that Lukas would stay in California through the end of the semester and then stay with me for the summer. I had already decided not to teach summer school this year. That gave me unlimited time to work on my writing and take care of Lukas.

"And Lukas was ok with that plan?" Pat asked.

"More than you might imagine," I replied. Pat wasn't aware that, just before Lisa's death, Lukas had asked if he could stay through the summer. I was slowly becoming more aware that Lukas liked having someone who looked after him and cared for him. And that I was a person who could do that for him.

I took the last sip of my iced coffee and got up to leave. "I better find out where he is and what he's up to," I said. He could be anywhere, but I had a sneaking suspicion that he was at the Top of Topanga, reflecting.

After saying our goodbyes, I got into my car and sat silently for a moment. *Lukas is my responsibility now*, I thought. There was no fallback position.

TOPANGA CANYON BLVD

When I returned to the house, the sliding doors to the deck were open, meaning that Lukas was home again. I found him sprawled out on the sofa, in his usual position, snacking on corn chips. He was staring at the TV. I looked at it and asked my usual question: "What are you watching?"

Lukas smiled up at me. "British soap opera. Hold on, let me rewind it. This scene will remind you of someone."

On the show, British Soap Opera Stepdad was having a meaningful conversation with British Soap Opera Teenage Stepson about an affair the stepson had with his teacher. The teacher was also dating the stepdad—yikes. What was Lukas implying here? Maybe we needed to have the boundaries talk?

Lukas could sense what I was thinking and laughed. "No, no, not that. The dynamic. The dynamic." I figured I'd humor him and watched from my position behind the sofa. He often found many interesting life lessons in TV shows.

Stepdad: You spelled meticulous wrong.

Stepson groans.

Stepson: Oh, the irony.

Stepdad: Your life's not a screw up, you do know that mate.

Stepson: Nothing gets past you, does it?

Stepdad: This last year, it's just been a setback.

Stepson: I've cut myself off from my mates.

Stepdad: Still got Liv, Noah.

Stepson: Failed my exams.

Stepdad: Yeah, but—

Stepson: And I nearly lost you.

Stepdad: Never.

Stepson smiles.

Stepson: So much has gone bad, it's made me start to realize, it was wrong.

Stepdad: So, college, fresh start.

Stepson: I just want a normal boring life again.

Stepdad smiles.

Stepdad: Normal boring life. How I love those words.

Stepson: I'm sorry.

Stepdad: No looking back.

Then, Stepdad and Stepson were interrupted by someone who appeared to be the Grandfather. He was apparently aware of Stepson's recently-resolved plight, and shared his thoughts with Stepdad and Stepson. It was a happy ending for all.

The scene transported me back to the summers of my early teenage years. With my dad working all hours of the day and night, and my mother teaching summer school, I typically spent my days at my nana's house in Encino. An Englishwoman, Nana Whitmore had easily transitioned from a hardscrabble early life in the Yorkshire dales to a relative carefree existence in suburban Los Angeles. She was a gifted baker; her house always smelled like fresh-baked brownies and scones. Nana was my best adult friend. She loved board games, and we'd play everything from Monopoly to checkers for hours on end. No matter which game we played, Nana would always find some way to sabotage her play to make sure I won.

Whatever we were up to, though, everything stopped at 11 AM for Nana's "story," *As the World Turns*. For an hour every day, Nana and I were transported to the small Midwestern town of Oakdale, Illinois, to drop in the lives of the Hughes, Stewarts, Snyders and Ryans. Some characters, like Dr. Bob Hughes and John Dixon, were doctors; some characters, like Emily Stewart and Molly Conlan, were reporters; others, like Margo and Hughes and

Hal Munson, were cops. Add in assorted lawyers like Tom Hughes and Jessica Griffin, and an assortment of children, and you had a stereotypical Midwestern town.

But it was not a normal boring life for the Oakdalians. They were involved in stories that seemed centered around the seven deadly sins. Some characters had illicit affairs; some characters were involved in shady business dealings. Other characters, like Steve and Betsy, or Tom and Margo, were deemed to be "super couples." Steve and Betsy seemed particularly tortured: each story revolved some effort to break them up. In the end, though, they always found their way back to each other, and happiness prevailed. I was mesmerized.

At the heart of Oakdale was the town matriarch, Nancy Hughes. Nana told me that Nancy had been a character since the beginning; she would often be seen serving coffee in the Hughes family kitchen, while various characters would drop by and share their troubles with her. Nancy always had solid, sage advice, and when a troubled character left her kitchen, they were ready to face another day. She reminded me of Nana. When I left Nana's house, I always felt better.

The daytime TV landscape was littered with soap operas. Some viewers were searching for a guiding light; some viewers had only one life to live; others checked into General Hospital. Eventually, I figured out the significance of the title of Nana's story: that no matter what happens, the world still turns.

In hindsight, I realized that my interest in writing stemmed from watching As the World Turns with Nana. Sure, some of the stories were unrealistic—I mean, how many surprise kids could James Stenbeck have? Throughout each show, Nana would give me her stream-of-consciousness take on what was happening on screen. I would try to argue why it might have been better for businesswoman Lucinda Walsh to not hire rapscallion Craig Montgomery as her new associate. While she always let me win at games, Nana would always win these arguments. After all, she had more experience with the real world turning than I did.

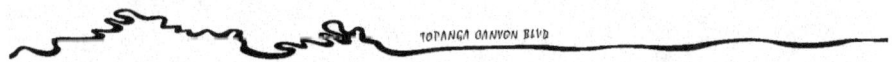

Another episode of the British soap opera Lukas was watching had started, with a Range Rover driving through the English countryside. I came back from my reverie.

"So, you're not dating a teacher," I quipped. My voice cracked as I tried to say something funny.

Lukas just looked at me. "Dude, you're an idiot," he said. I sat down on the sofa next to him and he quickly snapped a selfie of us. We looked at the photo together; I saw Lukas had tears streaming down his cheeks. He gave me a big hug.

"I just want a normal boring life," Lukas proclaimed. I'd had a boring life until now. It had been anything but boring since Lukas arrived. I was happy to provide whatever kind of boring life Lukas wanted.

THREE

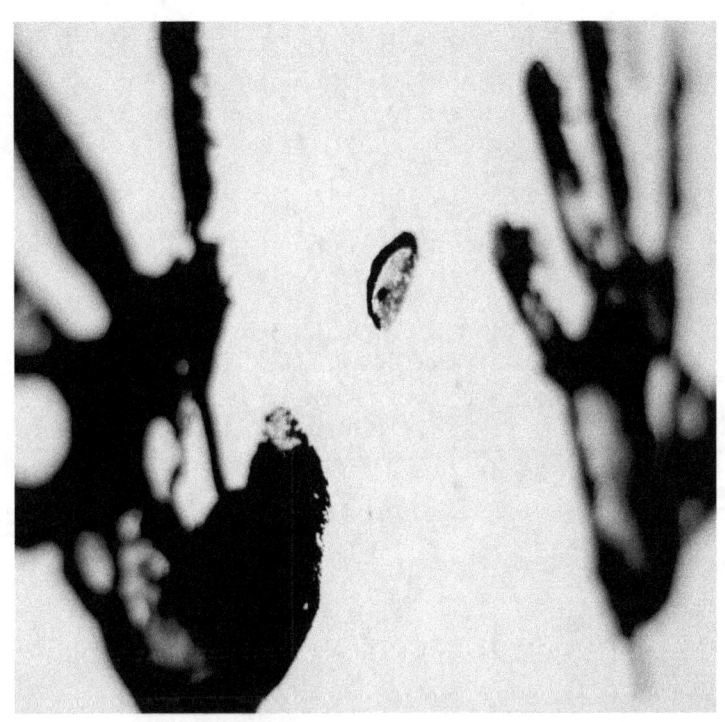

Monday morning came far too quickly for both Lukas and me. There were stacks of tests on my desk, ready to be graded. Lukas had a week of work to complete, and he needed to start preparing for final exams as well. In Miami, Lukas had always struggled academically, mainly because he rarely took his schoolwork seriously. While his teachers there cared, they never seemed to be able to break through to him. For some reason, his attitude toward school had changed since he had been in California. Maybe it was the new start, the new environment. He still struggled at times, and he still displayed his goofy charm as a student, but he had started applying himself at last. He really wanted to do his best.

When I came downstairs that morning, I was surprised to see Lukas already in the kitchen, eating cereal. He was fully dressed and his backpack hung over the back of his chair.

"You're up early," I commented. Usually, I had to drag him out of bed.

Lukas said that he was having trouble sleeping. He figured he would may as well just get up and get ready for school. I reminded that our first stop of the morning was to meet with his academic advisor. We needed to discuss a plan of action for Lukas to make up his missed work. Lukas dismissed the need for a meeting, saying he would be just fine.

We made good time to Malibu High through the Santa Monica Mountains. Lukas took his usual pretzel approach to sitting in the passenger seat, curling up in a tangle of long limbs. He fiddled with the radio, apparently displeased with any of the musical selections on Sirius XM. Then he traced the early morning moisture on the window with his finger.

I pulled into an empty faculty parking space. It felt good to be back on campus. Lukas grabbed his backpack and got out of the car as I pulled my briefcase from the backseat. He asked again if we really had to meet with his academic advisor, Mrs. Sato. I told him to humor me—and her.

Mrs. Sato was sipping coffee in her office when we arrived. She'd been at Malibu High forever. Mrs. Sato wore her hair in a tidy bun and dressed in a series of perfectly contrasting prints. Her workspace was precisely organized: piles of file folders were stacked neatly on her desk and in folder holders on the credenza behind her. If they ever needed to recast Ms. Darbus in a new version of *High School Musical*, she would be perfect for the role. I hoped she wouldn't ask Lukas how he was doing.

"Good morning, Lukas, Noah," she said politely. She searched for his folder on her desk for a moment before looking back up at him from behind her oversized glasses.

"How are you?" And there it was. Lukas just rolled his eyes. Deep down, he felt that if he made it through his first day back, he could tolerate all the questions about his emotional state going forward.

"I'm fine. Thank you for asking," he replied dryly. At least he wasn't being sarcastic. I thought maybe he'd become immune to the question.

Mrs. Sato first offered us a comprehensive review of Lukas' academic performance since he started at Malibu High. Chemistry was his best class; English Literature his worst. While Lukas had a sharp, analytical mind, he clearly didn't enjoy reading and, as a result, his reading comprehension suffered. Lukas often said that he'd read a few pages, get distracted or disinterested and then move on to some other assignment or non-school activity. Mrs. Sato was aware of this from reports from Lukas' teachers. She suggested that Lukas undergo some appropriate testing to identify any learning issues. Lukas just rolled his eyes again. He hated tests to begin with. Now his teachers wanted to test him to see if he had trouble taking tests.

Mrs. Sato showed us a little grid with all of Lukas' classes and the essential assignments for each class. "Since your academic performance has been adequate this semester, and considering the circumstances of your mother's death, we are prepared to waive your final exams," she said. "You will be exempt from them with no penalty. You will, though, need to complete the work you've missed."

I expected screams of joy but Lukas simply said, "Thank you, but no." I was dumbfounded. So was Mrs. Sato.

"Wait—you *want* to take your final exams?" she stammered.

"I appreciate the offer," he said "but I'll take them."

"Are you sure?" Mrs. Sato and I said in unison.

"Remember what you told me when I got here?" Lukas asked me. "'You buckle down, do your schoolwork, and do your best.'" I was stunned. Doggone it, the kid did pay attention to me.

"Well, there you have it, Mrs. Sato," I said. "Lukas will sit for his exams."

Lukas smiled. "You know, in England, they say 'revise an exam.'" He'd been watching that British soap opera way too much. "See, I'm learning!"

A week later, the pile of ungraded physics final exams on my desk had grown substantially. I was a notoriously slow grader. Like Lukas, I was easily distracted by outside influences, but had never been formally assessed with ADHD. It didn't matter, anyway. I always managed to get my work done, and done well.

I stared at the pile in front of me. I'd typically count the number of exams or lab reports I had to grade. Then, after grading for what seemed to be a while, I'd do a recount to see "how many I had left." I always assumed I had made a major dent in my pile; in reality, I'd only graded three or four papers. When it came to final exams with mathematical problems, I'd look at the numerical answer first. If that was correct, I'd assume the process to get there was correct as well. It was a cheap shortcut to grading volumes of papers. Just like looking for the right buzzwords in short answer responses.

The phone at my desk rang and the caller ID said it was Mrs. Sato. I was tempted to just let it ring, in fear that she was calling once again to see how Lukas was doing, but answered it anyway.

"Noah, its Elizabeth Sato. How is your grading going?" Ah, the standard Malibu phone call first line: "How's your blank going?" Someday, the ghost of Gene Rayburn was going to show up to see if we could match Brett Somers and Charles Nelson Reilly. According to Elizabeth, there was a potential problem with Lukas' English exam. A student had reported that she thought Lukas was trying to sneak a look at her essays. After Lukas' prior proclamation that he wanted to do well on his exams, I found it strange that he would resort to cheating. But then again, desperate times often called for desperate measures, and Lukas had resorted to desperate measures before. I thought he might have cheated if he thought he was going to fail. I knew he didn't want to disappoint himself and I'm sure he didn't want to disappoint me.

Elizabeth informed me that there would be a meeting in her office at 3 PM. Just what I needed.

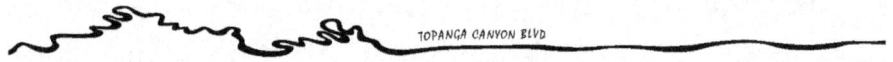

TOPANGA CANYON BLVD

Lukas was sitting alone at a picnic table in the quad. Being that it was exam week, the quad cleared out quickly in the afternoon, as students went home to study or hit the beach to hang out. Lukas was just frustrated. He sketched so hard in his notebook that the pencil point almost went through to the next page.

Emery sat down beside him. "Heard you're accused of cheating on the English Lit exam," he said.

Lukas smiled. "Word gets around fast."

"It's supposed to. It's high school."

Lukas assured Emery he hadn't cheated. Emery asked him if he had maybe stretched the boundaries of honesty just a little bit.

Lukas broke his pencil in half. "You don't believe me either?"

"C'mon dude, maybe you just took a little peek at her paper?" Emery responded calmly.

Lukas tried to remain calm as well. "Give me some credit. I told you that I wanted to do my best on my exams. I told Noah that. I told Mrs. Sato that. I could have taken the easy way out and gone with the exemption. But I didn't."

Emery nodded in agreement. "That's a valid point. When do you have to go pay the piper?"

Lukas wasn't sure who the piper was or how much he'd have to pay. He often took statements too literally and never seemed to be able to decode a metaphor.

"3 PM meeting with Noah and Sato," he said. "Should be fun."

"Just be honest," was all the advice Emery could offer.

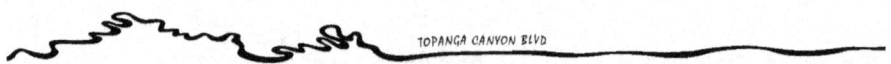

I leaned back in my chair and stared at the ceiling. Every time I thought things were finally settling down with Lukas, something new popped up. It seemed like that was what being a parent was all about.

Pat entered and saw the frustration on my face. "Something wrong?"

"Sato called. Apparently, Lukas has been accused of cheating on his English Lit test."

Pat looked surprised. "I thought he said he was going to prepare and do his best."

"That's what I thought as well," I commented dryly.

"Another real parenting test for you," she replied. I was sure Pat was ready with some advice so I just went ahead and asked.

"Any advice? I'm thinking I should believe him."

"I think that's a wise idea. He may not admit it publicly but he is in a very fragile state right now."

"Don't you think that's being overly dramatic?" I asked. To me, it seemed like another version of "how are you doing?"

"Don't you remember how you were after your own mother died? You don't think that is still affecting you today?"

Pat was right, as always. I reminded myself, once again, that I myself had failed to deal with my issues of loss when my mother died, and I couldn't help but think that, in some way, that failure had turned me into the loner teacher determined to save every student. I'd done my best to give Lukas the time and space that he needed. But maybe I needed to make sure he had the time and space to talk. Funny how I always seemed to return to the same thought bubbles.

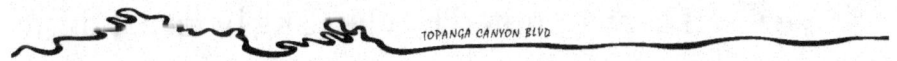
TOPANGA CANYON BLVD

Olivia the waitress smiled when Lukas and I approached the hostess station at the Canyon Diner. She gave him a big hug and said that she had heard about his mother passing. Apparently, there were no secrets in Topanga. Lukas thanked her for not asking how he was doing.

We took our usual table in the back by the bug zapper. Olivia knew us well as customers: after she served us water, she said she'd be back with our usual in a while.

"Thanks for going to bat for me with Sato," Lukas began. He appeared genuinely thankful.

"That's Mrs. Sato," I corrected him. As an aspiring writer and as a teacher, word choices always mattered with me.

"Thanks for going to bat for me with Mrs. Sato," he said dutifully.

"It's what I do. Go to bat for you," I said. Lukas knew the girl had recanted her accusation.

Lukas frowned. "Wait—you think still I cheated, don't you?"

We've all been tempted by cheating before. I think that deep down, part of me doubted his innocence. I hesitated.

My momentary silence was all Lukas needed to release the emotions he had bottled up over the past few weeks. He slammed his water glass onto the table so hard, it smashed into a million little shards. The other patrons turned around and stared in shock.

"No one ever believes me," he bellowed, bursting into tears. Pat had warned me this was going to happen.

Before I could reply, he stood up and realized everyone was staring at him. This embarrassed Lukas even more, and made the tears flow even faster. He bolted out of the diner.

This was not the time to give him space to be by himself. I got out of my chair and ran after him, apologizing to the other patrons as I tripped over chairs in a vain attempt to catch up with him. I finally found him in front of the Topanga Post Office, across the street from the diner. He sat on a bench that advertised Topanga's Do It Wright Painting. He was still crying, just not as much as before. I realized I had only one chance to "do it right."

I resisted the temptation to start talking immediately and tell him that everything would be ok. I knew it would be a long time until things would be ok for Lukas, so I just gave him a hug. He squeezed me so tightly that I thought he was going to split me in half.

"I'm sorry," Lukas mumbled. "I didn't mean to embarrass you."

I figured I'd try a little humor. "You didn't embarrass me. You embarrassed yourself!"

Lukas whacked me in the arm. "Jerk," he moaned.

Maybe a different kind of humor would work. "Should I ask you how you're doing?"

"Do I *look* like I'm doing ok?" He pushed the Chalamet hair out of his tear-streaked face.

I did feel sorry for him. Being abandoned by your parents, shipped across the country, and learning your mom had died suddenly—none of that was easy. Of course, there were other kids at Malibu High with much more serious problems and much more difficult lives. But Lukas was my main concern now.

"You talk, I'll listen," I said, my tone turning serious.

"I'm not sure what you want me to say," Lukas muttered.

"What do you want to tell me?"

"I didn't mean to embarrass you," he said again.

I reminded Lukas that was a repeat. Repeats didn't count.

Lukas was finally direct. "I feel like my head is in a vice," he said.

That was an interesting analogy. "Say that again," I requested.

"I feel like my head is in a vice. Like all of these stresses are crushing me."

I thought I might turn the conversation back on him. "What could *I* say to make you feel better?"

"Nice abdication of parental responsibility." Lukas was turning sarcastic. He was very good at that.

He slowly stopped crying. "I guess I just don't know what to do," he continued, after a long pause.

"It's ok if you don't. You're just a sophomore in high school," I said. "I felt the same way when my mom passed away."

"So how did you handle it?"

"Well, I did what everyone told me not to do. I bottled up my emotions. I had a hard time trusting people with how I felt."

"And why was that?" Lukas was starting to see his response to his mother's death was eerily similar to mine.

"Because people I thought were my friends in middle school turned out to not be my friends at all."

A look of confusion came over Lukas' face. "What happened in middle school? Were you bullied?" The kid hit the nail on the head. I struggled with how to respond.

"Care to share?" he prompted. I was surprised that the focus of the conversation had turned back to me. But I knew that to help Lukas overcome his present difficulties, I had to give him a deeper insight into my own difficulties growing up. It seemed like the "right thing"—the "dad thing"—to do.

"Middle school was rough for me," I began. "Friends that I trusted with my personal feelings decided to make those feelings public. I was clumsy, and I was socially awkward too. I was smart, but that wasn't enough to overcome my other shortcomings."

"Middle school must have been tough then," Lukas said. "I won't complain anymore."

"You're not complaining," I replied. He really wasn't.

"Tell me more," Lukas said, distracted from his own struggles.

I hadn't shared these thoughts of mine in years, but now the words were flowing. "As I got older, I found myself with fewer friends. I hated sharing my feelings. When my mom passed away, I chose not to share my emotions with anyone, even my own dad. He worked a lot, so I found myself on my own a lot. It became easier and easier for me to be by myself."

"Is that why you became a teacher?"

"Pretty much. I knew there were kids out there alone, who needed help. I wanted to help them."

"So, I messed up the picture, then?"

I told Lukas that I was surprised when his mom asked me to take him in for a few months. I was tempted to tell him that I had viewed it as an opportunity to save one more student, but thought it better to phrase it in a different way.

"Not at all. Part of me was tired of being alone. Part of me was tired of having no one to talk about at the faculty lunch table. Part of me was tired to listening to all their family stories."

"Now I get it. I was just a means to an end." Lukas said this sarcastically, but smiled to let me know he didn't really mean it.

"Maybe you are. More importantly, maybe—just maybe—I needed someone like you in my life. Right at this moment in time."

"And do you think I needed someone like you in my life, right at this moment in time?"

I smiled. "We're sitting next to each other right now, aren't we?"

I suggested that we head back to the Canyon Diner. I had no doubt Lukas was hungry for his spaghetti and meatballs.

"Thanks for sharing all that," I said as we stood up. I'd managed to help him climb down off the emotional ledge he'd been sitting on just an hour before. I was proud of myself for doing so well with Lukas. I just never expected to do it at the Topanga Post Office!

I heard Lukas' stomach growl. "You have to promise me something," I told him.

"What's that? Not to eat you out of house and home?"

"You already do that."

Lukas smiled, a little shyly. "You really don't have to say anything. I get it."

I messed up the Chalamet hair and smiled back. "No looking back, Lukas. No looking back."

FOUR

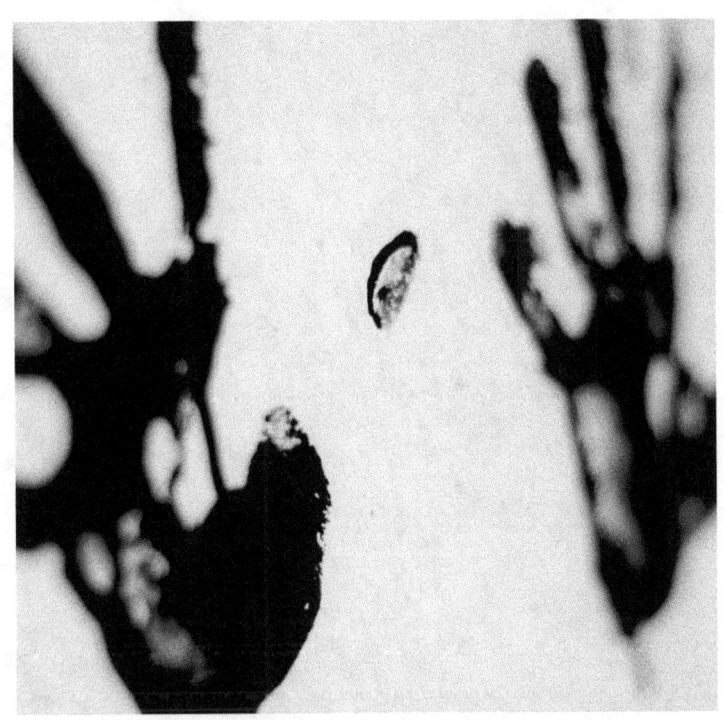

The school year ended quietly for Lukas and for me. I typically taught summer school, but considering how the last few months had transpired, I thought it best not to make a long-term commitment. In addition, my scriptwriting had taken a back seat to my other responsibilities, and I knew I needed to get back on track with that as well.

I sat nursing a midnight mocha iced coffee at Malibu Coffee + Tea when my dad Matt walked up. He'd just finished a round of golf. Free to do whatever he wanted—retired life must be awesome! He sat down next to me with a cup of coffee: black, no sugar.

"How's summer vacation treating you?" he asked.

I looked at my watch. "So far, it's been awesome."

"Where's Lukas?"

"Summer vacation? He wouldn't be anywhere else but home, fast asleep."

I then pulled out Lukas' report card and showed it to my dad. He smiled as he looked it over. "The lad did a good job, considering."

There was only one C on his report card: English Literature. Lukas had struggled in that class all semester. His highest grade was a B+ in chemistry. Most importantly, though, Lukas was satisfied with his academic performance. His analysis was spot on, as well: "More Bs than at a beehive."

"What's Lukas doing for the summer?" my dad asked. "Working here?"

"No, he's got a job working at the Malibu High Summer Soccer Camp." The job involved teaching and coaching children ages six to eleven. It would certainly be more meaningful for him than bussing tables at Malibu Coffee and Tea.

"When does he start?" Dad continued. I said I was pretty sure Lukas had a week of freedom before the job started.

Dad nodded. "Could I give you some parenting advice?" he asked. I mentally braced for this. My dad would have been wise, at times, to take parenting advice from others rather than offering it himself.

"What advice would that be?" I asked, figuring I'd be diplomatic.

"Remember that road trip that we took after your mom died?" Dad asked.

I remembered it well. It was a valiant attempt at a vacation, but it turned out to be an epic disaster. Chevy Chase's vacation trip to Wallyworld was more successful.

Dad suggested that Lukas and I just get in the car and drive up the coast. Right away.

"But I haven't made any reservations anywhere," I said.

Dad rolled his eyes at that. "For once in your life, just get out and do something without planning it months in advance. Topanga will survive without you being here for a day or two."

He was right about that. Still, I felt resistant, and Dad recognized my frustration.

"I have an idea," he said. "A friend of mine works in admissions up at UCSB. Why not drive Lukas up there for a college visit? Gets you and him out of here. Gives him a little bit of the college experience."

That seemed manageable to me. Besides, there had to be a number of hotels in Santa Barbara listed on TripAdvisor.

"Sounds like a plan," I said.

TOPANGA CANYON BLVD

I returned home. Lukas was up, sprawled on the sofa watching TV.

"5, 4, 3, 2..." he chanted.

"I never figured you for an *iCarly* fan," I remarked.

"I think this is your favorite episode, the one with the pirated DVDs," he said. It was. It had my favorite line: "Wow, this store is so convenient."

"*I know you see. Somehow the world will change for me. And be so wonderful,*" Lukas sang along with the theme song.

"Did you shower yet?" I asked, interrupting him.

"Are you serious? It's only 10."

"Then get off your butt and shower. Put some clothes in a bag. We're going up to UCSB for a day or two."

"Wait, what?" Lukas was shocked.

"You heard me, we're going away. Consider it an early college visit."

"But dude, where's the spontaneity coming from?" he demanded. "You really planned this months ago, didn't you?" Lukas knew spontaneity was not in my wheelhouse.

"Nope. My dad just suggested we just get out of town."

Lukas grinned. "Ok, I'm in." He leapt over the sofa and bounded upstairs. Ten minutes later, he was back downstairs, freshly showered with his packed Adidas backpack by his side. "Ready to go!" he announced. He was one of the most adventurous people I'd met. We still didn't have a hotel reservation, though.

I was more procedural in my approach to travel and to life. This time, though, I needed to be spontaneous. I avoided the temptation of downloading the "Guide to Santa Barbara" App on my phone, and quickly packed a suitcase. Like my mother always taught me, though, I packed an extra pair of underwear and an extra pair of shoes—just in case I had an accident and just in case it rained.

It took no time to load up the car. An hour after I'd left Malibu Coffee + Tea, the Audi was packed and we were on our way.

Andrew Gold's *Lonely Boy* came over satellite radio. Lukas quickly changed the channel. "Ain't a lonely boy no more," he declared.

The drive up the 101 was a quiet one. Lukas alternated between falling asleep and staring out the window. I think he enjoyed the peace and quiet. It had been a wild couple of weeks.

As we passed the Camarillo Outlets, Lukas bolted up in his seat. "So how long are we staying? What are we going to do?"

"My dad arranged for us to get a tour of the UCSB campus. You're going to have to start thinking about college soon," I reminded him.

Lukas chuckled. "Do you really think I'm college material?"

"As goofy as you think you are, I know you're pretty smart. Give yourself a little credit."

"You certainly have, dude."

"That's why I became a teacher."

"To put up with goofs like me."

"No. To let goofs like you know someone believes in you."

With that, the rear tire on my Audi blew out.

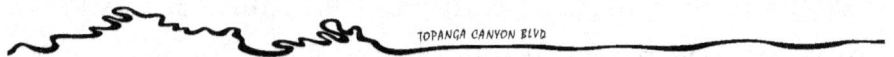

TOPANGA CANYON BLVD

I sat in the service area of the DCH Audi of Oxnard, waiting for the technician to repair my vehicle. I loved auto dealership lingo. It was never "your car," always "your vehicle."

Lukas bounced back in after exploring the nearby area for an hour. He was growing impatient. "Dude, what happened? How long is this going to take?"

"Nothing major, just the blown tire. It's almost done. Where were you anyway?"

"Across the street," he said, gesturing vaguely.

I looked out the window of the service department waiting room at the plaza across the way. "I doubt you were at Premier Furniture."

"On the other side of the highway. At the chapel."

This surprised me. "What were you doing there?"

"Reflecting. I took some pictures of the sanctuary."

Well, this was interesting. I'd never known Lukas to go to church, nor had we ever discussed religion. However, I did recognize a solemnness to him at his mother's funeral.

Meanwhile, Lukas swiped through the photos on his phone. "Isn't the architecture cool?" he said, showing them off to me. He seemed proud of his photographic accomplishments.

"Lovely little chapel," I said. I suggested that if Lukas was so enamored with the chapel, he could become a priest.

"That's not happening. Church photographer, maybe. But priest, no way."

I looked through the photos. Many were very good. He was actually rather talented.

"Who are we going to meet at UCSB?" Lukas asked, still impatient. "If we ever get there."

"Selin," I said. "She's the director of admissions. She's going to give you a personal tour."

"That's nice of her. Man, your dad knows everyone." Lukas plopped his black Converse sneakers on the table, causing the selection of outdated *Popular Mechanics* magazines to scatter. "Don't you think it's a little early to start thinking about college?" he asked.

"It's never too early to start thinking about the future," I reminded him.

"I have trouble dealing with the present. Please don't give me one of your teacher pep talks."

I knew Lukas was referencing the British Soap Opera Stepdad and Stepson. "I wasn't going to do that," I replied calmly. "I *was* going to say that whatever you choose to do, you'll have my support."

Lukas seemed pleased by this. "I know how you plan everything. I figured you'd have my future all planned out too."

"The sun shines equally on everyone. You just need to find your place in the sun."

Lukas took a deep breath. He'd never heard anyone say that to him before, and he understood what I meant.

Just then, the service advisor looked up from the computer and announced, "Mr. Whitmore, your vehicle is ready."

Our appointment at UCSB was at 10 AM the following morning. We arrived at the UCSB campus early, but it took us a while to find Cheadle Hall, and we were about 10 minutes late for our appointment. We might have been on time if Lukas hadn't decided to fiddle with the GPS. It also didn't help to have him keep saying, "Is *that* the building?" I hated being late for appointments.

My dad's friend Selin was waiting for us by the entrance. She was a stately woman, wearing a long wool coat with a bright UCSB Admissions pin on the lapel. Her hair was perfectly coiffed. If they ever needed a body double for Kitty Carlisle, Selin would be a suitable candidate.

"Noah Whitmore?" she asked. I nodded. She looked professional; she sounded professional. I doubted that Lukas would be able to charm her.

"And you must be Lukas." Selin looked directly at my cousin. "I hear you might be interested in UCSB."

"I just finished my sophomore year. I'm not sure what I want yet," he said. At least he was direct.

Selin asked about Lukas' grades and, again, he was refreshingly honest. His first three semesters in Miami had been a disaster, but he'd improved significantly during the spring at Malibu High. When she asked about extracurriculars, Lukas explained that he was passionate about soccer and had been playing since he was 8.

Selin handled the lack of extracurriculars diplomatically. "I might suggest you find an additional area of passion," she said. With that, she suggested we go on a walking tour.

Lukas thought the campus was "spacious" and listened attentively as Selin talked about each building, as well different activities and different majors on campus. Her talk was sprinkled with interesting admissions department facts about the number of students, their country of origin and their success rates after graduation.

We made our way over to Storke Field. The UCSB men's soccer team was on the field for an early summer practice, and Selin introduced Lukas to the coach. After a few moments' discussion, the coach walked Lukas over to the side of the field. Selin stayed next to me.

"Matt said Lukas has had some difficulties over the past few months," she said quietly.

I explained that Lukas had been living with me since January and that his mom had recently passed away. I looked over at the soccer field and saw Lukas was in goal, fielding kicks from the UCSB players.

"He really is quite talented, isn't he," Selin observed. "Any idea of a major?"

"I don't think he has a clue."

"This will be an important year for him to get his act together."

"He's starting to realize that. And he's starting to focus on that. But he definitely doesn't want anything handed to him."

Lukas trotted off the field back over to us. "I'm sorry," he called out. "The coach asked me if I wanted to try being in goal. I couldn't resist." In just a minute, Lukas seemed to have matured from a goofy teenager to a young adult.

"Are there any departments you'd like to learn more about, or buildings you'd like to see, or professors you'd like to talk to?" Selin asked.

Lukas furrowed his brow for a second before asking if we could visit the education department.

I almost gasped. "You want to be a teacher?" I asked.

"I have no idea, dude," Lukas admitted. "Just something I've been thinking about."

I patted him on the back. It was sweaty. He smiled.

"I've got a good role model, you know," he said.

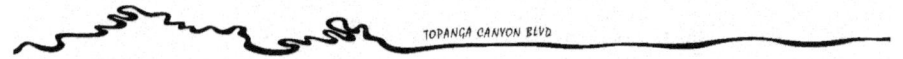

TOPANGA CANYON BLVD

After an exhaustive tour of the UCSB campus, Lukas and I returned to the hotel. He decided he wanted to sit out by the pool for a while, so I grabbed a book and joined him. Lukas' pale skin was not particularly suited for the California sun. He slathered on almost an entire bottle of SPF 45 sunscreen and then passed the bottle to me, before placing his Beats headphones over his ears and just staring off into space.

I made some progress with my book, but in my mind, I kept reliving the last six months. I looked over at Lukas, and for the first time in a few weeks, I felt he looked truly calm. Then it hit me. With every day that passed, I became more and more responsible for him. It was an awesome responsibility, one that I had not taken lightly.

After some time had passed, Lukas shifted in his deck chair, took his Beats headphones off and turned to me. "I'm starving," he announced. This was accompanied by his usual rubbing of the stomach, Lukas' universal sign of hunger.

After a quick shower and a change of clothes, we headed to the hotel lobby. The front desk clerk, a chipper young woman named Claire, suggested Brophy Brothers at Santa Barbara Harbor. Lukas was in the mood for "oceanside dining" and joked that the harbor location would allow him to "sea" the ocean. I winced and the desk clerk groaned at Lukas' feeble attempt at humor.

"I'm used to it," I told her.

She laughed. "I'm sure you are!"

We walked down Shoreline Drive and turned onto Harbor Walk. The Walk was teeming with families, young couples on dates, and Santa Barbara teens skateboarding. Lukas and I merged into the crowd inconspicuously. We knew no one else's story that evening and no one knew ours. There was something to be said about being an unknown in a sea of strangers.

The dinner at Brophy Brothers was worth the wait—and the investment. Lukas gave his crab cakes "two enthusiastic thumbs up," while my baked clams rated five stars. I was glad that Lukas had retired his sometime champagne tastes for the evening and opted to not order the lobster. I did find it difficult to say no to him! Throughout his life, he'd never wanted for anything except for love and appreciation. Love I could give him for free. Everything else seemed to cost a fortune. Still, he was worth it.

As we left the restaurant, Lukas had a spring in his step. Apparently, the crab cakes had given him more than enough energy to retain his bounce for the evening. He explored the front of the Santa Barbara Maritime Museum and then bounded over to the railing to watch a seal making noise on a rock. He soon felt the need to imitate a seal barking, and then turned to me and asked if his impression had earned my "seal of approval." I could only groan.

Lukas turned quickly on his Converse sneakers and spotted a tattoo parlor hidden around the corner. He looked at me, dead serious, and asked, "Could I get a tattoo?"

I knew this wasn't a good idea. I shared my concerns with him.

"You're such a stick in the mud," he groaned. Lukas argued that he was going to be a junior in high school and "everyone has a tattoo." That was never a compelling argument for a parent or a teacher. I tried "if everyone jumped off the Brooklyn Bridge," but that fell on deaf ears. I'm sure there was some deeper-seated reason why Lukas wanted a tattoo, but he wasn't telling me.

Lukas promised that his tattoo would be respectful; he already knew what he wanted. It wouldn't be a tattoo of Metallica or some other heavy metal band.

I knew I had to put my foot down. I told Lukas that, no, he would not be getting a tattoo. Lukas huffed, mumbled something about how I don't understand teenagers, and sat down in a funk on a nearby bench. I was sure that other parents had faced similar challenges. I also knew that if I failed in this challenge, I might lose Lukas' trust.

I opted for the buddy-buddy approach and sat down next to Lukas. "Do you want to talk about it?" I asked. He huffed again, stood up, and walked over to the harbor overlook. His whole body slumped against the railing.

I followed him. I asked him if he wanted ice cream. He slid away from me. It was clear I wasn't going to win this argument. I suggested we head back to the hotel. Lukas shoved his hands deep into the pockets of his shorts and shuffled along, keeping his head down. I chose to maintain the silence between us. And so did he.

TOPANGA CANYON BLVD

Our hotel room was stuffy when we returned. Lukas kicked off his sneakers and laid down on the bed. Before I had the chance to say anything, Lukas slipped his headphones on and started air drumming. Any possibility for conversation for the evening appeared to be over.

I grabbed a book from my briefcase and went out to our room's balcony. The sun was slowly setting "in the west." I always felt the Pacific had a calming influence on me. That's why I found my bench at Will Rogers State Park to be a perfect place to reflect, and why I found the deck at Malibu Coffee + Tea to be the perfect place for meaningful conversation.

I resisted the temptation to reflect on how much life had changed for Lukas and me over the past six months or so. I found myself doing that far too many times lately. I'd also had no communication from Peter in the past few weeks. It was becoming increasingly apparent to me that Lukas would be my responsibility for a lot longer than a semester and a summer. With my tattoo decision tonight, I felt like I had blown the present; I needed to focus on the future.

I looked back into the room and saw a lump on one of the beds. Lukas was motionless; he had fallen asleep.

I had made no progress in my reading and put the book down on the small patio table. Before long, I too fell asleep.

TOPANGA CANYON BLVD

A chilly breeze blew off the Pacific, through the volleyball nets on the beach and finally hit me in the face like an unexpected slap from an irate girlfriend. I jumped out of my chair and looked at my watch. It was 9 AM. We should have been on the road back to Topanga by now. I hated oversleeping.

I looked into the room and saw one of Lukas' gangly legs and Converse sneakers sticking out from under from the white hotel blanket. It must have been a rough night of sleeping for him; the blanket had more twists and turns than a complex *Law & Order* episode.

It was tempting to get Lukas up now. I felt so "parent-y" saying that to myself. I decided to let him sleep in. I showered, dressed quickly and headed out to Starbucks to get us both some breakfast.

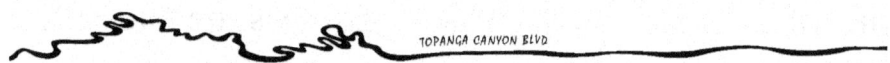

TOPANGA CANYON BLVD

The morning fog had burned away and our room was filled with bright sunlight when I returned with two ham and cheese croissants and two Grande white chocolate mochas. I knew a croissant would not even begin to satisfy Lukas' morning appetite but it would be enough food to keep him going until we could stop for a more substantial, Lukas-approved breakfast on the drive home.

I knew by the pile of used towels on the bathroom floor that Lukas had already showered. He apparently needed more beauty sleep, though, before getting fully dressed. Lukas had fallen back to sleep in just his boxers. He looked peaceful; I hoped that his anger from the night before had faded away.

I shook him. Lukas stirred and mumbled something about being hungry. He rolled over and I saw the bandage on his left shoulder.

"Lukas Jaden Whitmore." I'd invoked the full name. Now he was fully awake.

"What is this?" I could feel the anger building in me. I knew what he had done. This seemed like a bad Silver Spoons episode.

"It's a bandage," Lukas said sarcastically.

"I know that. Is there a tattoo underneath that bandage?"

"There could be." More sarcasm.

"Do you want to explain how you managed to get a tattoo?" I could feel the anger building in me.

"I snuck out last night and went back to the tattoo parlor. They hooked me up." I didn't even think to ask how he, a minor, got the release form signed. I was that angry.

"After I told you no tattoos?" I wondered how Edward Stratton would have reacted if his son Rick had done the same thing.

Lukas smiled. "Take a look at it."

I peeled back the bandage. The tattoo was small and it was blue. It was a re-creation of our hand prints on the back of his bedroom door.

A tear came to my eye. I really wanted to be mad at Lukas. But I just couldn't.

Lukas sensed I was melting. I was such a softie. "You want one?"

"I'm not sure teachers should be getting tattoos." Besides, part of me was still mad at him.

Lukas reached under the bed to a small paper bag. He pulled out a small square of plastic and placed it in my hand.

"There you go."

It was a temporary tattoo. Lukas then peeled the tattoo off of his shoulder. "Got ya!"

The look on my face must have been priceless. I pushed Lukas back onto the bed. "I hate you."

"The guy at the tattoo parlor whipped up a whole batch of them just for me. I paid for it with your credit card, of course." Of course he did.

"I'll get you back for this." I knew my attempt at payback would pale in comparison.

Lukas gave me a big hug. "Love ya, dude."

FIVE

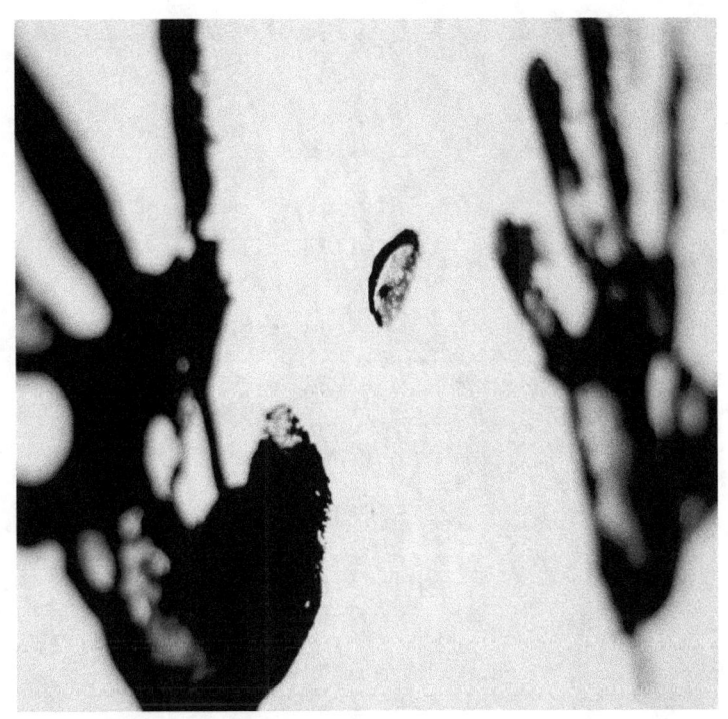

The trip to Santa Barbara was just the break we needed after a very long semester. Lukas returned home with renewed energy, ready to start his summer job as a student aide at the Malibu High Summer Soccer Camp. The job would give Lukas more financial stability than his previous gig at Malibu Coffee + Tea, and would have more meaning than collecting dirty coffee cups or washing dishes in a kitchen. He was genuinely excited about this opportunity, saying he felt like it gave his summer "purpose." I was thrilled when anything gave him "purpose."

Meanwhile, I picked up a few tutoring gigs each week. While I found the one-on-one aspect of tutoring to be boring, it required very little planning and no grading. Besides, an hour's tutoring in Los Angeles could bring in $250. Since Lukas was my responsibility for the summer, the extra income would help keep him fed and clothed.

Lukas woke up early for his first day of work. In the kitchen, he fidgeted with his glass of orange juice, eventually knocking it over and staining the pristine white table cloth. He immediately apologized.

"Nervous?" I asked, sopping up the juice with a towel.

Lukas nibbled at his plain bagel. "Why would you think that?"

I looked down at his feet. "Because you're wearing two different sneakers."

Lukas looked down. One was black, one was blue. "Oh," he stammered. "L-like you've never done that."

"Nope! Never have," I said briskly. Truth was, I probably had.

There was a knock at the door. My dad waved at us through the glass before entering.

"Is there someone here ready for his first day of work?" he asked brightly. Lukas grinned and raised his hand before heading upstairs to get his gear.

Dad saw the tattoo on Lukas' shoulder as he ran up the stairs. A quizzical look came over his face. "You let him get a tattoo?" he asked me, bewildered. I explained how he had asked to get one in Santa Barbara but I had not acquiesced. I told my dad the tattoo was temporary.

"You must be humbled, in a way," my dad commented.

I shrugged it off. "He didn't tell me what his tattoo was going to be," I said. Truth was, I'd been very touched when I saw those blue hand prints.

Dad smiled. "You two seem to be bonding pretty well," he said. To be honest, Lukas and I had a closer relationship than my dad and I had had when I was growing up. Dad's job as police captain and then police commissioner kept him very busy. He had always made sure that he was present for every one of my milestone events in high school and college. It's just that he often wasn't there for the smaller events in between. That's when I really needed him. Of course, I'd learned to live with it.

I had promised myself that with Lukas, I'd be there for every moment. Still when my dad offered to drop Lukas off for work so I could focus on my vacation, it was hard to say no. Lukas already knew I'd give him some lame pep talk or speech on his first day, and he was ok when I promised to pick him up at the end of the day, instead. I could give him my speech then.

Lukas came back downstairs properly dressed for work, wearing matching sneakers at last. Pinned to his official polo shirt was his official name badge: *Lukas Whitmore, Student Aide.* He looked professional, or as professional as one could for a summer soccer camp employee. I took a picture of him in his new uniform.

My dad smiled and gave him his seal of approval. "Ready to go, sport?" he asked

Lukas saluted. "Yes, sir!" And off Lukas went for his first day of work. I sat down on the deck for my first day of vacation.

With no summer school classes to teach and no physics tutoring on the agenda for the day, I had the morning to do whatever I pleased. I felt like a retiree as I headed off to Malibu Coffee + Tea. Pat had suggested we meet for coffee.

"How was the trip to Santa Barbara? How'd Lukas like UCSB?" she asked, nursing the cup of hot coffee in her hands.

"He liked it a lot," I said. "He was pretty interested in the education department."

Pat looked surprised. "Maybe he wants to be a teacher. Just like you."

I had this vision of Lukas in front of a class of enthusiastic students who loved to learn. It excited me. "Might explain why he's working as a student aide this summer!" I said.

"Have you considered counseling for Lukas?" Pat had her counselor hat back on.

I thought back to when my own mother died. My dad had suggested I try counseling to deal with my own issues of loss. I'd passed on it, instead trying to deal with those issues in the way I knew best: by myself. Lukas wasn't the type of kid who would enjoy sharing his feelings with a stranger. He didn't even like doing it with people he knew.

"I mentioned it to Lukas. He didn't seem too interested. He's an independent spirit, as you know."

Pat smiled. "I meant counseling for you."

"For *me?*" I was surprised she suggested that. "I don't think I need counseling."

"Maybe counseling isn't the right word," Pat said. "Maybe a support group. After all, you lost a close friend. And you have to support a young man who just lost his mother."

I didn't really like airing my personal troubles in front of a group of strangers, but I promised Pat I would think about it. I thought it might ok if the group was from the old Bob Newhart show: crazy Mr. Carlin, insecure Mr. Petersen, clueless Mrs. Bakerman. Then I might just be the normal one.

Lukas said goodbye to my dad at Malibu High. He felt excited about the summer and his job as a student aide. He was also proud of himself. He'd applied for and gotten the job all by himself, with no help from me, my dad or anyone else.

As Lukas walked toward the soccer field, he spotted Emery standing by the school swimming pool. Emery caught sight of him and waved, excited to see his buddy. "Dude. You're back. How was the trip?"

"Pretty awesome," Lukas said, brushing a hand over his eyes.

"Are you crying?" Emery rarely saw his friend get emotional.

"Dude, don't get me started!" Lukas laughed. He felt he had cried more in the past few weeks than in his whole life.

Emery gave Lukas a hug. "Wanna hang out after work?" he asked. "It's been a while."

"Noah's picking me up today. I don't want to disappoint him," Lukas said. He knew how important it was for me to be there in my dad role on his first day of work.

"You better get your ass to work, then! There'll be mobs of little kids here for soccer lessons before you know it."

Lukas grinned. "Thanks, man. You're a good friend."

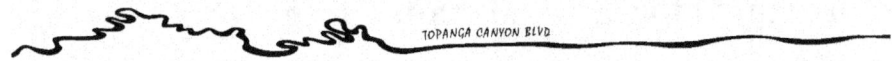

Lukas' first day was incredibly busy. One minute he was demonstrating basic soccer skills to eight-year-olds. The next minute he was monitoring six-year-olds as they took their bathroom break. Lukas thought he had boundless energy, but these kids had it in spades. He felt like an old man. Now he knew how I felt at the end of a long day of teaching.

The day flew by very quickly. Lukas was charged with corralling all of the campers from their various activities for pick-up at the circle in front of the school. As the group jostled together impatiently, Lukas' supervisor asked him to do one last sweep. One aspiring soccer star seemed to be missing, but this was not unusual on the first day of camp.

Lukas did one more walkthrough looking for the camper who was still unaccounted for: Liam. Lukas remembered him. Liam was the gangly eight-year-old with no soccer skills whatsoever. Every time he went to kick the ball, he would send it well out of bounds, essentially halting any forward progress. The other campers soon became frustrated with his lack of game. Liam had spent most of his afternoon on the bench, watching the more skilled players battle it out the field. Privately, Lukas thought that the kid was more suited for arts and crafts camp.

On a hunch, Lukas headed out to the quad. He had seen Liam sitting there alone during lunch. Lukas remembered his first day at Malibu High some six months ago, sitting alone in the quad as the new kid in school. Then he spotted Liam sitting alone at a picnic table. His uniform was still clean; Lukas doubted that the kid had even broken a sweat the whole day. Liam was sitting with his head in his hands.

"Hey, Liam," Lukas called out. "We're waiting for you over at pick up."

Liam lifted his head. He had clearly been crying.

"Hey, sport, what's wrong?" Lukas asked, surprised.

Liam remained silent.

"Not a good day?"

Liam looked Lukas directly in the eye. "Are you serious? Did you see me out there? I stink."

"You had some skills," Lukas said.

"My only skill was kicking the ball out of bounds."

Lukas remembered his first day playing soccer. He had had no skills either. "You've never played before, have you?" he asked.

"Do I look like it?" Liam replied snarkily.

"Why'd you sign up for camp then?" Soccer camp really seemed like an odd choice for Liam.

"My mom thought it would be a good way for me to make friends," Liam sighed. "We just moved her from Cupertino." Lukas could sense that the kid really didn't like living here quite yet.

"I grew up in Miami," Lukas shared. "I moved here back in January. I'm living with my cousin, and it was hard for me to fit in too when I first arrived in Malibu."

Liam didn't seem too interested in the parallel story, but he was fixated on Lukas' athletic prowess now. "How'd you get so good at soccer?" he asked, sitting up straighter on the picnic table bench.

"A lot of practice. Hitting the field every day. If you want to get good at soccer, you'll need to practice too."

Liam's face crumbled a little. "I just want to be good at something. I'm not good at *anything*."

Lukas smiled. He was pretty sure he had the same conversation with his mom when he started playing soccer, and he remembered me giving him a similar speech when it came to academics. "Do you want to be good at soccer?" he asked, point blank.

Liam kicked the dirt in front of his feet. "Yeah. Well, maybe. I don't know."

"Did you have fun today?"

"It was ok." At least the kid was honest.

"Your mom's not going to let you drop this, is she?"

"Oh, no. I'm committed for the whole summer." Liam let out a loud, dramatic sigh. "I think the bench will be my new friend," he continued, tapping it with his finger for full effect.

Lukas offered him a deal. During their free time, Lukas would do some one-on-one skill work with Liam. He might never be a champion on the field, but at least he'd be able to compete whenever they played soccer in PE.

Liam smiled a little and said he thought that sounded like a good deal. Lukas patted him on the back. "Feel better?"

"Yeah, thanks, dude."

"OK, let's get you to pick-up then!" The two of them headed out of the quad toward the circle to meet

Liam's mom. Lukas could only smile as he reflected on their conversation. However small, Lukas knew what it meant to make a difference in someone's life.

TOPANGA CANYON BLVD

Lukas had texted me, saying that he was running late at camp and that Emery would drop him off for dinner. I waited patiently at the back table at the Canyon Diner for about half hour before he finally arrived. While he wasn't sweaty, he was definitely smelly from a full day's work, and needed a shower. I pinched my nose, making the universal sign of "you smell," and he just looked me and mouthed, "You too." I found his goofiness charming.

Lukas plopped down in the chair, his scrawny legs sprawled wide. "Dude, I'm beat," he said. "I don't know how you work all day."

Olivia came over and smiled at Lukas, who told her he was famished. "The kid worked his first full day today," I announced proudly. Lukas just rubbed his stomach, and Olivia said she'd bring a double order of spaghetti and meatballs.

"Why were you late?" I asked.

"I had a camper who didn't have a very good day. He has zero soccer talent."

"And what did you do? Point out his weaknesses and laugh at him?"

"Do you really think I'd laugh at a kid like that?" Lukas asked.

"Well, yes," I said. Sarcastic commentary was Lukas' middle name. It was mine, too. It served as a defense mechanism, and had worked well for me all these years. People would never reach your inner core if you didn't let them.

Lukas shrugged. "You have me on that one." He went on to explain Liam's saga: how he just moved here from Cupertino, how he had no friends, how his mom signed him up for soccer camp, even though the kid had no real interest in soccer whatsoever. Except for the lack of soccer skills, Liam's story could have been Lukas' story.

"I offered to give him some one-on-one work during his free time," Lukas said. "It felt like it was the least I could do."

I congratulated Lukas on his mature approach, and he smiled. "People like you have had faith in me," he said. "I thought it was time people like me had faith in others." He grabbed a piece of bread from the table and wolfed it down.

"Hungry?" I commented.

"Dude, I don't know how you manage to work eight hours a day. I'm exhausted." Lukas grabbed a second piece of bread. It was gone in a flash.

"Welcome to the real world, my friend."

Olivia arrived with our usual order: fish and chips for me, spaghetti and meatballs for Lukas. Lukas practically grabbed the dish out of her hands. "Someone must be hungry," Olivia observed.

"You try working all day. You try not getting a break to eat," Lukas moaned. Apparently, he was the only employee to ever work a full day without a meal break. Olivia just laughed and put the check on the table.

"Watch your manners, Lukas," I said.

"I'm sorry," he said reflexively.

"Not me. Her."

Lukas turned to his friend. "I'm sorry, Olivia."

Olivia smiled and mussed up the Chalamet hair. She then wiped her hand on her apron. "You sure did sweat all day, that's for sure!" she said before hurrying off to another table.

"So, seriously—besides a hectic schedule and no lunch break, how was your day?" I asked.

"I might ask how *your* day was," Lukas retorted, flipping the conversation back to me. "No teaching, no grading, no planning."

"I had coffee with Dr. Branigan," I began. "Then I spent the afternoon on the deck working on my script." It had truly been a relaxing day for me. I definitely needed it.

"Progress, dude! I like it."

I shrugged. I never did seem to make any real progress on my writing. I'd carry a draft of my script back and forth to school, thinking that made me a writer. Never mind that I never took it out of my briefcase! My goal was to have a final version by the end of the summer. One can definitely dream big.

"You told me about the troubled child," I said, changing the subject. "How did you like working in a teaching capacity?"

"I don't know about 'working in a teaching capacity,'" Lukas said. "All I really did was give some basic lessons to the beginners. Oh, and taking campers to the bathroom and cleaning up the snot from their noses. Not particularly glamorous."

"What did you do when a camper couldn't master the skill you were trying to show them?" I asked.

Lukas took a break from his spaghetti to respond. "I had them keep practicing. Or I showed them another way." He stopped and thought about this for a second. "Ooooh. I get it."

Lukas looked tempted to fling a forkful of spaghetti in my direction. "Get what?"

"I see what you did there. Always coming back to how awesome it is to be a teacher. That we are all teachers."

"After your interest in the UCSB education department, maybe you're thinking of a career in teaching," I suggested.

"Whoa, dude, don't get ahead of yourself," Lukas exclaimed. "I'm pretty far from picking a career for the rest of my life."

"I'm just giving you some guidance."

Lukas smiled. "You focus on your fish and chips. I'll focus on my future." He laughed before returning to his actual focus: dinner. He loved spaghetti and meatballs much more than talking about the future.

SIX

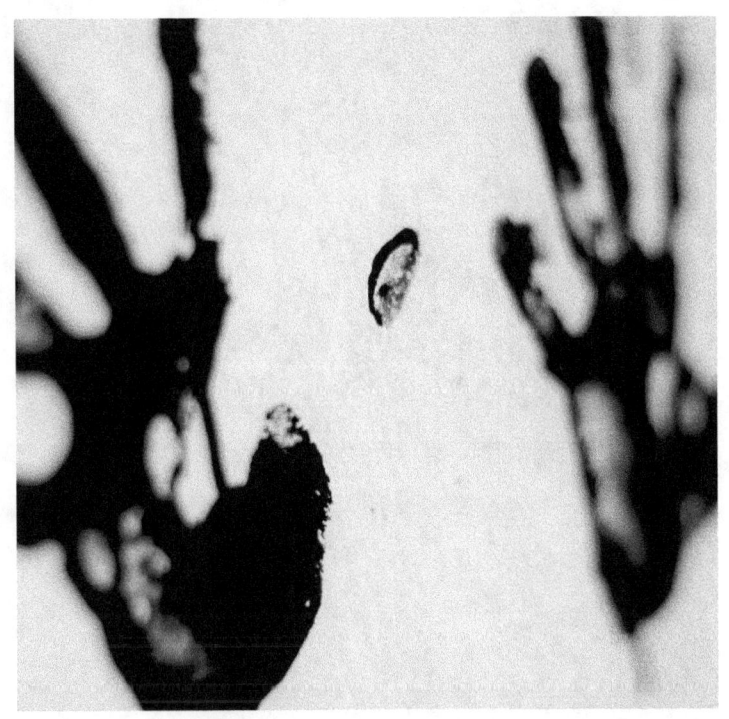

L ukas settled into the regular rhythm of being a student aide at soccer camp. He liked being responsible for campers and he liked teaching the campers basic and advanced soccer skills. He would often stay after work, volunteering to teach extra lessons at after-camp, or supervising late departures. Lukas had also become a "big buddy" to Liam, who, while not a gifted soccer player, was slowly improving his basic skills.

With all this time to myself, I was making significant progress on my script. Still, I found myself missing Lukas' sprawled-out presence on the couch, watching and commenting on some 1980s sitcom while tossing popcorn in the air.

Summer also meant it was time for my annual trip to San Francisco for the California Science Teachers Conference. Two of my session proposals had been accepted this year. I liked doing presentations as it gave me the opportunity to share the work of my students. But I hated attending conferences alone. If there was a request to "pair up" with another teacher during a workshop, I often felt like the odd teacher out. I always avoided the nightly socials and often found myself sneaking a meal into my hotel room, because I always struggled to make conversations with teachers I didn't know. I was the poster child for the introverted educator. Thankfully, Katie—Lukas' chemistry teacher and one of my favorite colleagues—was going with me.

A few days before my trip, my dad stopped by the house. I was putting the final touches on one of my presentations and did not particularly want to be interrupted. However, he *did* have a cup of coffee for me. I didn't want to dismiss this gesture so I welcomed him in.

Dad asked about my presentations and was interested in seeing them. I turned my laptop in his direction and went through my slides on the use of mobile data collection in physics. I felt pleased that he showed an interest in my work.

The conversation then turned to Lukas. "What are you going to do with him while you're away?" Dad asked.

Yikes. I'd never even considered who would take care of Lukas while I was away. I'd been on my own for so long that I didn't have to worry about someone else when I traveled; I would just pack my suitcase, lock the door and head to the airport. Having Lukas here added a new wrinkle to my travel plans.

"Any chance you'd want to watch him?" I asked. I thought Lukas would appreciate some one-on-one time with Matt. The two of them had bonded nicely since Lukas had arrived.

"You know I'd love to have the kid with me for a week, but I'll be in San Diego for a retired policemen's event. You'll have to find someone else," Dad said. So much for that option.

I mentally ran through the possibilities. Maybe Pat could look after him for the week. Or he could stay with Emery. Or—

"What if he went with you to San Francisco?" Dad suggested.

I rolled my eyes. "If you were a kid, would you want to spend a week at a teachers' conference?" Besides, I knew Lukas would not be able to get off work for a week, nor did I think he would want to miss work for that long. Lukas hadn't missed a day yet.

Dad agreed. "Why don't you let him stay here by myself?"

I was surprised by the suggestion. "Seriously? On his own?"

"It's a good way for him to learn responsibility," Dad said.

"Lukas needs to learn how to handle responsibility before he can take it," I countered.

"If you don't give the kid responsibility, how can he learn to handle it?" Matt responded. It was one of his circular arguments.

"I don't know. Lukas, living on his own for a week?" I replied, concerned about what might happen.

"From what you've said, he did a pretty good job fending for himself in Florida," Dad said, shrugging. That was true as well, I had to admit.

I had been thinking of this as a full week, but it was really only four days. Emery could pick him up for work and drop him at home. Pat could check in on him if necessary. I could ask Lukas to call me when he got home from work. My dad was right: this was a good opportunity for Lukas to learn some responsibility.

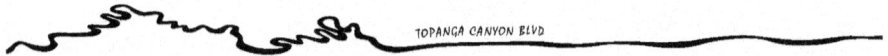

Lukas was thrilled that he would have the house to himself for four days. He promised me that he would check in daily and that only Emery would be allowed in the house. Even though it was out of my way, I dropped Lukas off at work before I headed to the airport. While he was grabbing his gear from the trunk, I got out of the car to talk to Emery.

"All ready for your big conference, Mr. Whitmore?" the young man asked.

"As ready as I'll ever be," I said. "You promise to keep an eye on Lukas?"

"I'll do my best. When do you get back?"

"Early Saturday morning."

Emery shook my hand. "I'll get him to and from work safely."

Emery had turned out to be a very good friend to Lukas. I appreciated that, and so did Lukas. He came up behind me and dropped his backpack and his Adidas duffel bag on the ground, feeling inspired to take a selfie with all of us.

"Call every day. And no parties," I reminded him.

Lukas groaned. "What am I, a child?"

Emery couldn't resist a jibe. "You're not a man yet."

"Har, har." Lukas turned to me. "I know. I know. No parties. Call every day."

I went to give Lukas a hug. "Dude, no hugs in public," he groaned, before extending his hand. I shook it, got in my car and headed off to the airport. Lukas was on his own now.

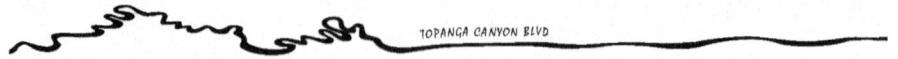

TOPANGA CANYON BLVD

The conference was a whirlwind of professional development. I liked having Katie as a traveling partner and as a co-presenter. We had a good rapport as colleagues and that made our presentations flow so much better. Attendees always gave our workshops high marks. Katie and I were pleased that our sessions were over-subscribed and that we had "reached our target audience." After each session, a group of teachers would approach us with follow-up questions and comments—another indicator of a successful presentation.

As we left our last session on Friday morning, I scooped up a pile of Marriott pens and notepads from the back counter. Free hotel and conference swag made for great prizes for in-class competitions. As I stashed them in my bag, Katie and I plopped down on a bench outside the conference room. It had truly been a long week. We were both ready to go home.

"What workshops do you want to go to this afternoon?" I asked Katie as I flipped through the conference program.

"I think I've learned enough science education for the week," Katie said. I agreed. I was tired of being in San Francisco. Katie added that she missed her kid; I missed my "kid," too.

"Why don't we get an earlier flight and head back tonight?" I suggested. It seemed like a reasonable solution.

"Let's do it!" Katie said. She immediately texted her kids about the change in plan.

I tried calling Lukas several times but he didn't answer. I was tempted to surprise him with my early arrival. Turns out, the surprise would be on me.

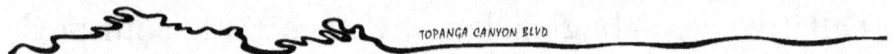

The week passed quickly for Lukas in the same way that it passed quickly for me. He was always tired after work, and after Emery dropped him off, he would grab some dinner and then crash on the sofa. He managed to keep the house neat and tidy, always cleaning up after himself, loading the dishwasher, and putting his dirty clothes in the hamper. Too bad he couldn't do that when I was home.

Friday afternoon had finally arrived, and Lukas was exhausted. He met Emery at the circle and tossed his duffel bag and backpack in the backseat of Emery's Mercedes.

"You wanna hang out tonight?" Emery asked.

Lukas was tired. All this actual work had worn him out. But it was also his last night unsupervised; he figured he might as well take advantage of it.

"Let's grab some Chinese, hang out, and watch Netflix," Emery suggested. Lukas thought that sounded like a plan.

Emery and Lukas stopped at Mr. Chow in Malibu, known as the "spin-off of the iconic Chinese landmark." Lukas loved the taste and smell of Chinese food. Heck, he just loved the smell of food. In no time at all, they got a bag packed with sweet and sour pork and hit the road.

The drive along the Pacific Coast Highway and up Topanga Canyon Boulevard was typically slow for a Friday afternoon. Lukas scanned through the channels on Sirius XM and finally settled on Channel 61, Y2Country. The sounds of Garth Brooks filled the car.

"What is this?" Emery asked.

"I don't know dude," Lukas said. "Lately, I've been listening to country lately. Noah likes it." Emery just rolled his eyes.

They pulled into the driveway and Lukas heard the familiar crunching of pebbles beneath the wheels of the Mercedes. He knew I was still away and that made him sad. He had grown accustomed to me being there whenever he got home. He knew I would be back from my conference the next day, though.

Once inside, the boys unpacked their food and spread it out over the coffee table. It had been a long day at work and they were both were famished. It didn't take either of them long to finish their food.

There was a knock at the door. "Come in!" Lukas yelled.

"You just let anyone walk into the house?" Emery asked, surprised. They turned around to see my dad standing there, who merely said, "Hey boys."

Lukas was surprised to see his "grandfather." Over the past six months or so, he really had come to see Matt as his grandfather. "I thought you were in San Diego," he replied.

Dad explained that he was on his way back from the convention. "Here to check in on us?" Lukas asked. Emery laughed.

"No. Now why would you think that?" Dad asked.

"Because it'd be easier for you to get to Calabasas from San Diego by taking the freeway, not by going through the back roads of Topanga," Lukas observed.

Dad rolled his eyes. "You're too smart for me, kiddo." He admitted he just wanted to see how they were doing. Scanning the coffee table, he took in the sight of all the remnants of the Chinese food. "Well— you are certainly well fed."

"Mr. Chow's. Can't beat it," Emery proclaimed. Lukas rubbed his stomach to demonstrate his satisfaction with the meal.

"What do you guys have planned for the night?" Dad asked.

This was one of the times Lukas preferred to be a homebody. "We're just going to hang out. Watch Netflix."

Matt seemed satisfied with their answer. "I'll leave you guys to your fun," he said. "If you need anything, just let me know."

"Noah will be back tomorrow," Lukas reminded him. "I think we're good. But thanks for coming by." With that, Dad headed out the door.

Emery grabbed the remote and turned on the TV. He found the end of a rerun of *Family Ties* on a local channel. Just then, there was a knock on the door.

"Did you forget something?" Lukas hollered without looking. He turned his head to see Dr. Branigan standing there. "Ugh, now what?" he groaned.

"Hi, Dr. Branigan," Emery said, welcoming her. "If you're looking for Mr. Whitmore, he's still in San Francisco."

"I know. He asked me to come by," Pat said. Turning to Lukas, she added, "You weren't answering your phone."

Lukas pulled his phone from his shorts pocket. It had been on silent. He'd missed three calls from me.

"He sent you to chcck up on me as well?" he grumbled.

Pat rolled her eyes. "No—he wanted me to let you know he's coming home tonight. He finished up at the conference early."

"He coulda just texted me."

"You weren't answering. And I was driving by." Pat always delivered information in a very direct, "I'm a psychologist" sort of way.

"Did he say what time his flight was getting in?" Emery asked.

"No, he just said he'd be back tonight."

Lukas was a little disappointed to lose out on one more night of independence. Part of him was looking forward to having me back, though. "Consider this message delivered. We've been behaving," he added. "Enjoy your evening!"

Pat wished them a good evening and headed out to her car.

"If you wanna get going, you can. Especially with Noah coming home early," Lukas suggested as he turned to Emery.

"Nah, I'll hang with you until he gets back."

They turned back to the TV, where another episode of *Family Ties* was in progress. Emery clicked on the channel guide.

Lukas read the description. "*4 Rms Ocn Vu.* When Mallory damages the car, Alex rents out the house during homecoming to raise money for the car repairs. Chaos ensues." He groaned. "I've seen this one before."

Emery laughed. "I haven't. You wanna watch something else, though?"

Lukas didn't respond. Onscreen, Alex P. Keaton watched in horror as a college student entered the living room with the kidnapped Crawford College

Kangaroo. Alex, Mallory and Jennifer were shocked when Steven returned home early.

The scene was soon interrupted by yet another knock on the door.

"Now who is it?" Lukas asked, annoyed.

Emery got off the sofa and opened the front door. Maverick—one of Lukas' fellow camp counselors and a senior at Malibu High—stood there with several of his buddies. In his hand, he held two six packs of beer.

"What are you doing here?" Emery asked Maverick. Most people thought Maverick was kind of a jerk.

"Heard there was a house party tonight," he announced.

Lukas looked over. "You heard wrong dude," he said, still annoyed. Fake news traveled fast in Topanga.

"Where's your hospitality?" Maverick asked, all innocence. "We know your dad isn't home."

Lukas opened his mouth to reply, but then shut it again. He had been about to explain his relationship with me, but decided it wasn't worth it. He was pretty sure Maverick wouldn't care. "Ok," he said, crumbling. "You guys can hang for a little bit and then you gotta get out of here."

On the TV, Alex P. Keaton could be seen pushing the unwelcomed guests out the door.

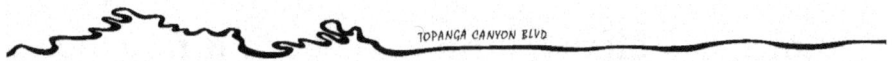

TOPANGA CANYON BLVD

Lukas felt a splash of water on his face. Opening his eyes, he looked around in confusion, still feeling groggy. He knew his body was oddly arranged on the sofa. More water hit his face.

"Wake up." He heard my voice. It seemed distant. Then more water, and a light slap on the cheek.

Lukas sat up on the sofa. It took him a minute to get his bearings. He realized I was home, and slowly looked around the living room. Empty beer cans and snack bags were littered all over, along with a completely empty vodka bottle. There was a crack in the glass of the sliding door. A framed photo of Lukas and me was on the floor, shattered. Lukas looked at the clock. It was 2 AM.

"Would you like to explain all of this?" I asked. Lukas knew I was angry. I rarely got angry with him.

"I can explain. I think," he said. He seemed shocked at the scene.

"Let's hear it."

Lukas grabbed his head. This must be what a hangover felt like. "Could I have a cup of coffee first?" he asked.

"How about an explanation first?" I replied.

Lukas searched his mind for an explanation that would make sense. He knew there wasn't even a story he could make up that would sound plausible.

"Emery and I were hanging out. Your dad stopped by, then Dr. Branigan. We were just gonna watch TV. Some kids from summer camp stopped by. I let them in. I didn't know they'd invite more kids over."

"Uh huh."

"You gotta believe me."

I pointed to the cracked door and picked up a beer can, before leaning over to smell Lukas' shirt. It smelled like beer.

"I trusted you to act responsibly this week," I said icily. "I come home to the leftovers of a party."

Lukas started crying. "I'm telling you, it wasn't my fault. They just showed up."

"You didn't have to let them in. Or you didn't have to invite them over."

"I'm telling you, I didn't," he wailed.

My anger grew. "Let's start with this first. You're grounded."

"For how long?"

"Let's start with forever," I snapped.

"But that's not fair," Lukas groaned. Thinking back on the previous evening, he was starting to think Alex P. Keaton got off a lot easier.

I invoked the classic line used by teachers and parents alike. "Life's not fair."

"That's the best you can do?" Lukas seemed disappointed in me now.

I was tired from my trip and I didn't have the energy to find out the whole story. "Why don't you just get to bed and we'll talk about this tomorrow?" I replied.

As he pulled himself off the couch, Lukas gave me a dirty look. "Why don't you just get to bed and we'll talk about this tomorrow," he mimicked, followed by an expletive. I decided to let it go.

I was too tired to clean up—and anyway, I thought Lukas should be responsible for it. Maybe leaving the crack in the sliding door alone for a while would be a good visual reminder to him about responsibility. Then I looked down at the ground and saw the cracked photo of the two of us, and my heart sank. One of us blew it just now, and I wasn't sure which one.

SEVEN

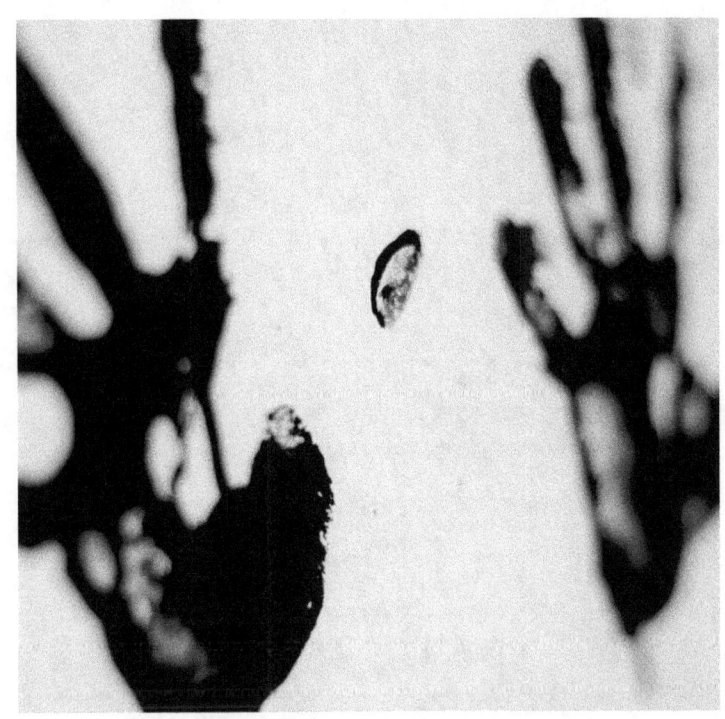

The sun rose over the Santa Monica mountains, shining through my window and waking me up. I was still tired from my week away, and frustrated with how I had responded to Lukas the night before. I should have been more patient in listening to Lukas' explanation. But finding a drunk teenager sprawled out on the sofa was a jarring experience—one I didn't want to have again.

I pulled myself out of bed, showered and threw some clothes. My stomach rumbled. I hadn't eaten since before my flight the night before.

Before I ate, though, I thought I should check on Lukas. I imagined he would have a whopper of a headache, being hungover. I knocked lightly on his door, not wanting to wake him up if he was asleep. Getting no response, I quietly opened the door and peeked in. His bed was empty, but not made. There was a note on the mirror, scrawled in marker. It read, "Sorry for last night. I'm at Emery's. I need to figure out a way to have you trust me."

I was saddened to read this, but I understood, and resisted the temptation to call him. I knew he would think I was checking up on him. I texted him, "Whenever you are ready to come home, let me know." There was no response. Still, I knew if Lukas was at Emery's house, he was in a safe space.

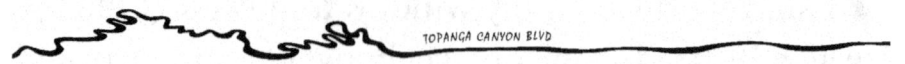

The parking lot of MC+T was surprisingly empty for an early Saturday. The air was crisp and very dry; the Santa Ana winds had arrived early this year. I opted to sit inside, sipping my midnight mocha iced coffee.

I heard a cough behind me and turned to see Pat standing there. "Hey, how was the conference?" she asked.

"It was ok," I replied. I could tell I had a glum look on my face.

"Just ok? You usually love them. What's the matter? No free pens at the Vernier booth?" Pat teased. She knew I liked my free pens. Free swag was the best part of a conference.

"The conference was fine," I said. "It was when I got home that was the problem."

She looked surprised to hear that. "What happened?"

"Lukas seems to have had a party last night."

"Seems to?" Pat asked. "Wouldn't you know if he had a party or not?" I explained the scene I encountered when I got home. "Sounds like a party to me," she said. "I only saw Emery there with him when I stopped by. What did he have to say in his defense?"

"That's the thing," I said, my guilt washing over me again. "I didn't give him a chance to say anything. I assumed the worst. I just grounded him straight away."

"That's a completely normal, parental response," Pat reassured me. "What did he say this morning?"

"Nothing. He'd run away to Emery's house. He said he needed time and space."

Pat smiled "That's a typical teen response," she said. "Flight or fight. Just give him some time, then he'll be back and you can talk it out."

I said nothing. I still felt glum.

"Did you ever think parenting was easy?" she asked me. "Teaching isn't easy. Parenting is even tougher. This is nothing."

"I suppose you're right. I just don't like making parenting mistakes," I said. I didn't like making mistakes in general.

Out came the psychoanalysis. "Maybe that's because you feel like your dad made mistakes," Pat mused. "You think if you make a mistake with Lukas, you're failing him."

My mind flashed back to the time my dad missed the annual Academic Awards ceremony in junior year because he was busy on a case. That was at least one time he failed me.

"I just feel like Lukas has been failed so many times before now. I don't want one more person in his life failing him."

"I know you try to be perfect in your teaching, and I know you try to be perfect in your life, but you can't be perfect in everything," Pat said. "You *will* make mistakes as a parent."

I nodded in agreement.

"I think it's something else, though," she continued.

"What's that?" I asked.

"I think you are afraid of losing him," she said. "I think you really like having him in your life."

That resonated a lot. I'd said to myself countless times that I could never have imagined how my life would change since Lukas—or how many times I'd promised myself I'd not say that to myself yet again. To hear someone else say it seemed to affirm it— make it real.

"He just needs time," Pat said confidently. "Lukas knows you'll be there for him." I hoped she was right.

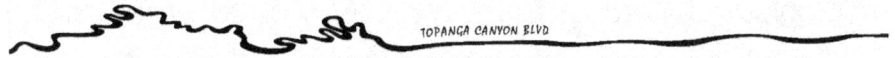

I sat on my favorite bench at Will Rogers State Beach the next morning. The Santa Anas were strong that day; I could smell a whiff of smoke in the air from a fire burning way up near Santa Clarita. The gusty wind brought a chill to the air.

I nursed my cup of coffee. I needed some perspective. I needed time to write. I'd pick up my journal, start to write, then put my pen, looking out over the ocean. I wasn't getting anywhere. Then I thought about how Lukas was doing.

I picked up my pen and wrote furiously.

Lukas woke up by himself in Emery's house. Emery's family had let him know they'd be leaving early for a family wedding in Santa Barbara. He felt alone. He missed my cheery smile greeting him in the morning.

Stumbling down to the kitchen, he rummaged through the refrigerator to find a bagel for breakfast, and popped it into the toaster. He was extremely hungry. A few minutes later he smelled smoke. He assumed that the bagel had burned in the toaster, but it had popped back out perfectly toasted. Maybe a neighbor was sitting on his deck smoking a cigarette.

After eating, Lukas sniffed his underarms and decided he definitely needed a shower. As he headed back upstairs, there was a loud banging on the door. Lukas just ignored it—probably a salesman or someone at the wrong house. His mom had taught him to never open the door to strangers. The banging continued as he kept going upstairs, followed by yelling. "Fire department. Anyone home?"

Lukas ran back down the stairs to the front door and opened it to find a fire captain in full gear standing before him. "Your parents home, son?" the man asked as he looked around the first floor.

Lukas thought it best not to explain his current living situation. "No, I'm here alone," he said.

"Grab your phone and a jacket. We're evacuating everyone in the area."

Lukas was puzzled, and nervously asked why. "A fire broke up on the next ridge and the winds are carrying it this way," the captain said. "We need to get everyone out. Now."

Sensing the urgency in the captain's voice, Lukas scrambled to put his sneakers on, throw on a hoodie and grab his cell phone. He hopped in the front seat of the fire captain's pick-up truck and they took off. In the rear-view mirror, he could see flames just beyond Emery's house.

An hour later, Lukas found himself sitting in a church hall, all alone. He was scared. He didn't know what to do. He didn't even have any clean underwear.

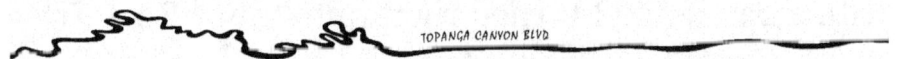

TOPANGA CANYON BLVD

Back at Will Rogers State Beach, an emergency alert on my phone indicated that a fire had broken out in southern Calabasas. Evacuations were taking place near Monte Nido. I kept writing, gradually noticing that the smell of smoke was growing stronger.

My phone chirped again. It was a text from Lukas. "Been evacuated to Calvary Chapel. Don't know what to do. Come get me. I'm scared."

My heart pounding, I debated what to do. Trying to get from the beach to Emery's house with a fast-moving fire approaching me was a dangerous proposition. But Lukas was alone, and scared, and he needed me.

I jumped in my Audi, threw my writing notebook in the front seat and roared out of the parking lot, noticing as I did that the air was starting to grow hazy with smoke. A sign I passed on the PCH said that Malibu Canyon Road was closed. My only option was to take Las Flores.

A stream of cars was heading south on Las Flores toward the PCH. I was the sole car traveling north, which made me nervous. I reached the junction of Rancho Pacifico and Pluma. Pluma was blocked with a barrier so I turned right onto Stunt Road. The smoke got thicker and thicker.

Deep down, I knew this was a mistake, but knowing Lukas was scared gave me an adrenaline rush I had never experienced before. That rush pushed me to press forward, until it was almost impossible to see, and my car engine couldn't take the influx of smoke any longer. When my car finally stalled, there was no one around.

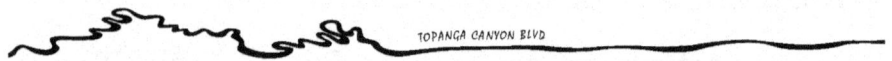

TOPANGA CANYON BLVD

In a scene reminiscent of a Friday cliffhanger on *Days of Our Lives*, I woke up in a mysterious room and mumbled, "Where am I?"

Looking around, I saw a number of hospital monitors. One was beeping quietly, while the others were silently displaying a continuous stream of data. I tried to move my arm but it hurt. My head hurt as well. I coughed repeatedly; my coughs tasted like smoke. I fumbled for the nurse's button and squeezed it. No one came.

TOPANGA CANYON BLVD

Lukas was sprawled out on two chairs in the waiting room, half asleep. My dad had texted Lukas to let him know I was in the hospital. Before Matt could send a patrol car for him, Lukas left Calvary Chapel and hitchhiked his way to me. He hadn't slept well since then.

A nurse came by to check on Lukas. "Morning, sunshine," she said calmly.

Lukas rubbed his eyes. "Morning. Did Noah wake up yet?" he asked.

The nurse said that I was still unconscious, before asking where Matt was. My dad had joined Lukas here.

"He went downstairs to get some food," Lukas said. "But I'm not really hungry." Lukas not being a hungry was a rare occurrence.

"Sweetheart, you should really go home and get some sleep," the nurse reminded him.

"I'm not going anywhere until Noah wakes up. He wouldn't leave me alone. I'm not leaving him alone," Lukas declared, struggling not to cry.

"That's very admirable. But you aren't going to be of any help to him if you're exhausted." The nurse had said this to many anxious family members before. They never listened.

Lukas sat up straight. "I'll make you a promise," he said. "If he's not awake by this afternoon, I'll go home and shower."

TOPANGA CANYON BLVD

How had I ended up in the hospital? I wondered. The last thing I remember was my car stalling on Pluma.

The door to my hospital room creaked open and a nurse peeked in. "You're awake," she said, coming inside.

"Yes, I am," I said. "Now where am I?"

The nurse fluffed my pillow. "You're in Malibu Hospital. You've had a bad case of smoke inhalation."

I looked down at the table next to my bed. There was a copy of the Los Angeles Times there, from today. Tuesday.

"It's Tuesday?" I asked, shocked.

"Yes, you've actually been unconscious for two days."

"What happened?"

The nurse explained that an ambulance had brought me in mid-day on Sunday. The paramedics had found me passed out next to my car. While I had ended up safe at the hospital, my beloved Audi had not. It had been barbecued by the quick-spreading fire.

"You should consider yourself lucky to be alive," the nurse said, jabbing a needle into my arm to draw some blood. "And lucky that the paramedics found you. Another hour or so and you might not be here today."

This was probably the first time I'd been confronted with my own mortality. That scared me. The nurse wrapped up her blood withdrawal and placed the vials in a little carrier.

"They'll bring some solid food in for you in a few minutes," she said. "We've been feeding you intravenously since Sunday." I was famished.

"I'm going to let you rest," she continued. "But there's a young man who's been waiting since Sunday for you to wake up."

My heart lifted. That meant Lukas was safe.

"Would you like to see him?" she asked, seeing my expression change. Yes, I would—more than she could know.

The nurse left the room. I rested my head back on the pillow, exhausted.

The door creaked open again a few minutes later, and I saw the Chalamet hair make its appearance. I'd never been so happy to see a head of hair in my life.

"Noah? You alive?" Lukas asked from the doorway.

"Yes, I'm alive. Come in!" I replied.

Lukas slipped into the room. He had on a hoodie, sweatpants, sneakers and no socks. He looked exhausted.

"Can I give you a hug?" he asked.

"Not too public for you?" I teased him. I was reminded of Lukas' unwillingness to hug me before I left for San Francisco.

"Oh hell no." He gave me a hug as best he could. I coughed in his face.

Lukas explained that he had been at Emery's house when the fire department arrived to evacuate residents. He had hitchhiked his way from Calvary Chapel to Malibu Hospital as soon as my dad had called him, not wanting to waste any time getting there. He had slept in the waiting room for the past two days.

"How did Emery's house fare?" I asked. He told me Emery had texted to let him know that his family's house had survived the fire unscathed.

Lukas started crying a little bit. "I'm sorry," he said. "This is all my fault."

"How is this your fault?" I asked. I didn't think this was the time to play the blame game.

Lukas kept crying. "If I hadn't let Maverick in. And that party hadn't happened. And I hadn't gotten drunk. And I hadn't run away. Then you wouldn't have had to come to get me."

I appreciated his honesty, but didn't want him to beat himself up. "There were a lot of hadn'ts in that sentence. Let's not discuss this now, ok?"

"But dude, you almost died. I almost lost you. It was my turn to act responsibly and I blew it."

"Yes, you blew it. But we should have talked it over, instead of me overreacting," I said.

"Does that mean I'm not grounded anymore?" Lukas asked.

"Oh no," I said dryly. "You're still grounded. *Forever.*" I needed to bring some levity to the situation.

Lukas' tears dried up, and he smirked. "I suppose I deserve that."

"Like I said, let's talk about this later."

"Do you want anything?" he asked. "I'll go to the cafeteria."

"The nurse is bringing me food soon," I said. "Is my dad around?"

"He'll be back soon," Lukas replied, passing me a cup of water.

"I want to ask you something," I said, after taking a sip.

"What's that?" Lukas had a concerned look on his face.

"What happened?"

"You mean like how did you get here?" he asked.

"No, with the party," I said. I knew how I ended up in the hospital.

Lukas groaned. "I thought you weren't going to ask about that right now."

"Anything else you wanna talk about instead? I have all the time in the world."

Lukas took a deep breath and began his explanation: Maverick had shown up at the house with some friends and some alcohol. Lukas made the mistake of inviting them in. Word spread on social media that there was a party at the Whitmore house. Before Lukas knew it, the house was packed with people.

"Did you drink?" I asked, I already knew he had, but I needed him to admit it.

"I did," he said.

"And did you think that was a good thing to do?"

"In hindsight, no. At the time, yes. I thought it'd be cool." Lukas said that everyone else was drinking, and he didn't want people to think he was a loser.

"Didn't turn out so well, did it," I said.

"Guess not," Lukas said, remembering the headache he had the next morning.

I went on to explain—kindly but firmly—why his drinking was a problem for both him and me in multiple ways. Lukas was surprised to hear that there could be serious consequences to a student party being held in a teacher's house.

Satisfied, I asked Lukas to lean over the bed closer to me. When he did, I messed up the Chalamet hair before grabbing his cheeks and looking him directly in the eyes.

"You learned your lesson?" I asked. Lukas nodded. "Then don't let this happen again," I said.

Lukas smiled. "Am I still grounded?"

"Oh yes. Forever."

Lukas groaned again at that. Then he smiled again. "I have something that might change your mind," he said.

He pulled something out from his bag. It was the photo of him and me that had been broken during the party, in a brand-new frame. He placed it on the table next to my bed before reaching in for another hug. "I want my greatest accomplishment to be making you proud of me," he said, growing emotional again.

I smiled at the photo and then at him. "Then you succeeded," I said. And then I coughed in his face.

EIGHT

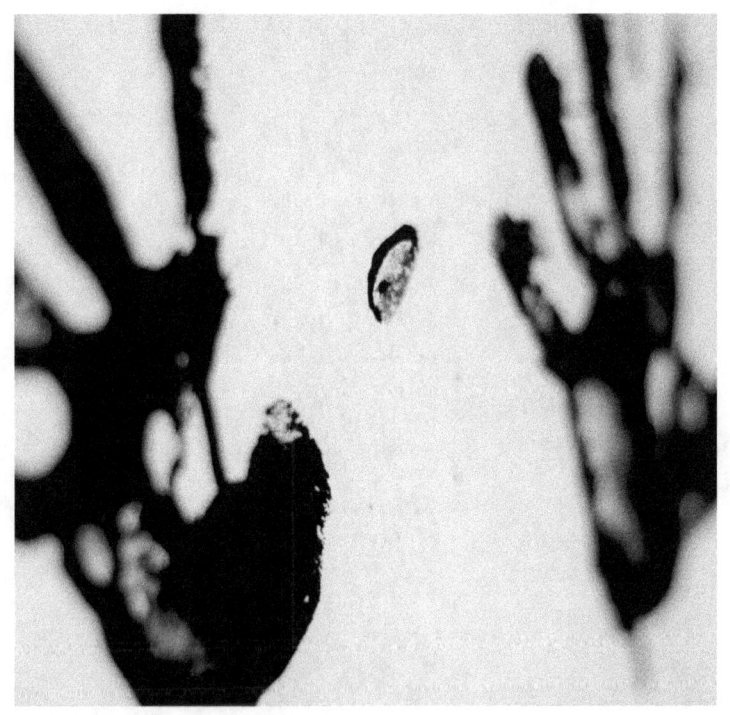

Iwas released from the hospital the following day with strict orders to spend the next two weeks recovering. Thankfully, as it was now summer vacation, I would be able to maintain my perfect attendance record. I thought I could manage being homebound for that long, as my beloved Audi was now toast in a vehicle compactor somewhere.

Lukas offered to stay home from work to help me out, but I promised him I wasn't so incapacitated that I couldn't take care of myself. He still felt deeply guilty over the party and everything that happened afterward. He offered to use his summer salary to pay for a new car for me. I assured him that the insurance would pay for it. Sure enough, Audi of Calabasas delivered me a new car by the end of the week.

Whenever Lukas was at home, he acted like a doting nurse. Pat explained that this was his way of working through his feelings of guilt. I didn't think Lukas had much to feel guilty about: to me, it seemed like a series of bad decisions on both our parts. Given my fragile condition, I appreciated being waited on hand and foot, but I could tell the poor kid seemed worn out from both soccer camp and taking care of me. I was tempted to tell him to just leave me alone, but I also knew he was just trying to be supportive.

We finally agreed that if I needed something, I'd ask for it.

My recovery also gave me time to work on my script. I set a reachable goal to have my final draft done within the two weeks. By the end of my first week, I found myself feeling much better. My cough had quickly subsided, and my energy was slowly returning.

That Friday, I heard Emery's car in the driveway and looked at my watch. It was well past 6 PM. I knew Lukas would be famished, but I didn't have the energy to cook dinner. Lukas slid open the door, dropped his gear on the floor and plopped down on his favorite chair, sighing in exhaustion.

"Rough day?" I asked.

"Yeah, those kids wear me out."

I had to laugh. "Yeah, I have *no* experience in that area."

Lukas looked around toward the kitchen. "Where's dinner?" he said.

I felt a little put-upon. "Is that all you can ask?" I replied.

"No 'how are you feeling? How was your day?'"

"Ok. How are you feeling? How was your day? Where's dinner?"

"Don't be a wiseass."

"Dude, you know you love it," Lukas smirked. "So, where's dinner?"

"I'm too tired to cook," I said. "What do you want? Pizza?"

Lukas wrinkled his brow before tossing his head back against the chair. The Chalamet hair was dripping in sweat, and a few droplets left his head and splashed against the wall. He turned to look at the crack in the sliding glass door.

"Why don't I make us something?" he asked.

"Besides a reservation?"

"Are you doubting my culinary skills?" he demanded. I couldn't help but laugh. The kid could toast a bagel, but that was about it. A full-blown dinner seemed like a long shot.

Lukas seemed determined to prove me wrong, though, and got up to poke around the pantry. "Will spaghetti do?" he asked. It wouldn't have been my first choice, but I wasn't about to stop him. I nodded and Lukas grabbed a pot from the cabinet and filled it with water. I resisted the temptation to give him cooking advice.

While focusing on the boiling water, Lukas asked me how my day had been. I'd made significant progress on my script and told him I was happy with how it was flowing. He nodded and asked if we had any spaghetti sauce. I directed him to the top shelf in the pantry. Dumping the contents of a jar into a bowl, he placed it into the microwave, entered some numbers on the keypad and hit start. He was telling me about how his charge Liam had been improving in his goaltending skills when the microwave started to shake violently.

"What time did you set for the sauce?" I asked, alarmed.

"Dude, I don't know—like ten minutes?"

"Turn it off," I said. The rumbling continued.

Lukas wasn't quick enough. The microwave belched as the bowl of spaghetti sauce exploded, causing the door to burst open and spraying Lukas with sauce. Thankfully it wasn't too hot.

"What the...!" Lukas exclaimed. His whole body was as freckled as his face. I had to laugh.

"Dude, it's not funny," Lukas said, glowering as he turned off the boiling spaghetti.

"Why don't you go clean up and I'll get the spaghetti on the table," I said. Even the Chalamet hair was freckled with spaghetti sauce.

Lukas headed upstairs to the bathroom while I drained the spaghetti. I checked the pantry for more sauce, but we were out.

Lukas quickly returned, still freckled with sauce. He clearly hadn't showered, just changed clothes. "No more sauce?" he asked.

"That was it, kiddo."

Lukas went to the refrigerator and grabbed some ketchup. He squirted almost the entire bottle into the bowl of spaghetti. "There you go. Instant spaghetti sauce." He seemed pleased with his culinary solution as he spooned some ketchup-sauced spaghetti onto my plate, then his.

"Cheese?" he asked.

I passed, then gave the spaghetti a taste. It was awful.

"How do you like it?" Lukas was hoping for a positive review.

"It has an interesting taste to it," I said. No restaurant would serve this.

"It can't be *that* bad," Lukas insisted. He shoveled a forkful into his mouth and almost immediately spit it out. "Dude, that's awful!" Getting up, he walked over to the trash can and began scraping his plate into it. "That's the worst spaghetti I ever had," he said.

"But it's still the best meal I ever had," I replied. Lukas smiled. He knew what I meant.

"Let's order a pizza," he said.

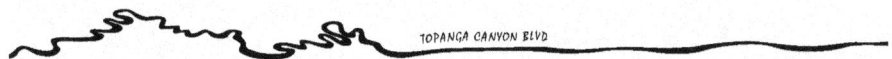

TOPANGA CANYON BLVD

Even though the doctors had ordered me to stay homebound during my second week of recovery, I decided I'd had enough of sitting at home, and offered to take Lukas to work on Monday morning. He double checked that I was ok with going out before happily accepting. I think he was just excited to have a ride in the new Audi.

The ride to school was quick. Lukas hopped out of the car, grabbed his gear, and headed off to work. As I turned to go, I was surprised to see Pat in the parking lot.

"What are you doing here?" I asked, turning off the car and getting out to greet her.

"I might ask you the same thing," Pat noted. "Aren't you supposed to be at home recovering?"

"I got tired of sitting around," I said. "I needed a break with my writing too." That was definitely true.

"I can understand that. How's Lukas doing?"

"Well, he's stopped doting on me, for now."

"Did you guys talk it out?" she asked.

I shrugged. "He knows what he did wrong. I know what I did wrong."

Pat jabbed her finger into my shoulder. "Good to hear."

I was still concerned about Lukas. "Do you think maybe you could talk to him?" I asked.

"I'll find him on my way to my office," she said. "Do you want me to tell him you asked me to talk to him?"

"You probably should." I knew Lukas didn't like subversive attempts to explore his emotions. It was always best to be direct with him.

We said our goodbyes and I got back in my car and headed home.

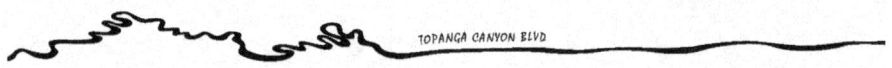

Pat looked around the quad until she saw Lukas sitting at a table with Emery, deep in conversation. Emery looked up as she approached and pointed her out to Lukas. "Hi, Dr. B.," Emery called out in his usual cheery way.

"Hey Emery!" Pat replied. "Lukas, could I have a word with you?" she added.

Lukas rolled his eyes. "Is this going to be another one of those 'how are you doing?' talks?" he grumbled.

"Well, to be honest, yes."

"And did Noah put you up to this?"

"He asked me to see how you were doing," Pat replied honestly. "We haven't planned anything, per se—he just asked me when I saw him just now in the parking lot."

Emery got up to leave, but Lukas motioned for him to stay. "What do you want to know? Just how I'm doing?" he said to Pat. "I'm doing fine."

Lukas was frustrated. "Look, I appreciate you checking in. But I really don't need any psychoanalysis."

"I didn't mean to intrude," Pat said diplomatically, getting up to leave. "Maybe we can talk later."

"Wait. Sit back down," Lukas said. As she did, Lukas recounted his "I threw a house party when an adult wasn't home" story. He reminded Pat that he'd gone through the apology tour with me many times.

"So, you're not feeling guilty anymore, then?" she asked.

"Well, I did almost get him killed coming to get me at the shelter. There's that." Lukas was always direct.

Pat looked Lukas directly in the eyes and raised an eyebrow sarcastically. "Oh. That."

"Yeah, that. *That's* what you need to talk through." All of a sudden, Lukas burst into tears and ran off. Pat had struck a nerve.

As they watched him go, Emery stood up and told her, "I'll go after him. I know where he's going."

"No, let me," Pat replied, also standing. "Where is he going?"

"Bottom of the stairs."

Pat worked her way through the campus until she reached the stairs that connected the upper campus buildings to the athletic fields below. It was a common place for students to go and reflect.

As she approached the top of the stairs, she saw Lukas sitting at the bottom with his head in his hands. Pat knew he was upset. She called out to Lukas as she walked quietly down the stairs, before sitting down next to him.

Lukas turned to her. "What do you want?" he asked.

"I think what I said really hit home for you," Pat replied. "Do you want to talk about it?"

"Everyone seems to say that to me a lot," he muttered, using his arm to wipe his eyes.

"Because people care."

"Why should they?" he demanded. Lukas always had trouble trusting people's motivations.

"Are you surprised that people care? Or are you surprised that Noah cares?" Pat asked.

"All I've done is cause him trouble," Lukas said, overlooking many of the high points of the last few months.

"And yet he still remains by your side," Pat reminded him. "Don't you think that means he cares?"

Lukas nodded in agreement. "I know. I just can't lose someone else," he said.

Pat listened quietly. "You mean, you can't lose him?" she asked.

Lukas started crying again. "Yes," he said. "I can't lose him."

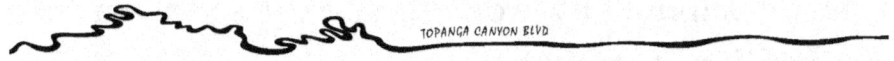

TOPANGA CANYON BLVD

The fresh air I got from taking Lukas to work was just the energy I needed to get my script back on track. By the end of the week, I'd finished my second draft and was pleased with the result. It looked professional: freshly printed with the required three brass fasteners.

I'd also finally made it to my last day of "house arrest." That in and of itself was reason for celebration. My dad arrived mid-morning with some coffee. I appreciated the gesture.

Our conversation turned to my health. In the same way that Lukas was tired of being asked how he was doing, I was tired of being asked how I was feeling. I assured my dad that I was feeling much better. I demonstrated this by not coughing for a solid ten minutes.

Dad spied the script on the coffee table. "So, this is finished?" he asked.

"Well, this draft is finished." I knew I needed to let it sit quietly by itself before attempting another edit.

"What are you going to do with it?" he continued. I really hadn't given it that much thought. I figured I would submit my work to several script writing competitions for amateurs.

We heard crunching in the driveway outside. I was surprised when Lukas walked into the living room, earlier than expected. He shook Dad's hand and smiled at me.

"You're home early," I remarked.

"How's work, son?" Dad asked.

"Summer's almost over. But it's been an awesome summer so far," he said. *That was relative,* I thought.

"So why are you home early?" I asked.

Apparently, the program was taking the campers on a field trip up to Zuma Beach. Lukas' sessions for the afternoon were cancelled and he was allowed to leave early for the day.

"What are we talking about here?" Lukas asked.

"Noah was just explaining how he'd finished his script and is going to be submitting it to some competitions," my dad said.

Lukas picked up the script and started flipping through it. "Can I read it?" he asked.

"I'd prefer that you didn't," I said. "Teachers and writers have fragile egos."

"Dude, how you gonna learn to be a writer if you won't let people give you feedback on your work?" Lukas asked. I think he just wanted to know if he was mentioned.

He did have a point, though. "Do you two really think you'd give me honest feedback?" I asked. "Or would you just tell me you thought it was good so you wouldn't hurt my feelings?"

Dad and Lukas looked at each other. "You have a point," Lukas admitted.

"Don't you have a friend who works at Paramount?" Dad was referencing my long-time friend Kate.

"I do, but I'm not sure she would give me honest feedback, either." I never liked using my friends for opportunities. I really was a poor networker.

Dad started swiping through the contact list on his phone and quickly made a call. "Kevin? Matt Whitmore here," he said. He walked out onto the deck, engaged in a conversation with this mysterious Kevin, leaving Lukas and I in the living room.

"What do you suppose that's all about?" Lukas asked.

"God only knows," I replied. My dad was always up to something, leveraging some connection for some advantage or opportunity. He soon returned to the living room and picked up the script. "Can I take this?" he asked.

"You mean, *may* I take this?" I replied automatically. I could only imagine what he was going to do with it.

"Stop being for a teacher for a minute," Dad admonished me.

"Who was that on the phone?" Lukas asked. Both he and I were curious.

"My friend Kevin. He works over at Sunset Gower."

"And why were you calling him?" Lukas continued.

"Oh no. Here it comes," I said. I was sure my dad had made some sort of deal.

Dad explained that Kevin was a major production executive at Sunset Gower. He had told him about my script, and Kevin was willing to read it objectively.

He stuffed the script in his pocket. "So, you'll let him read it?" he said.

"Do I have a choice?"

Lukas whacked me on the back. "That's the spirit!" he exclaimed.

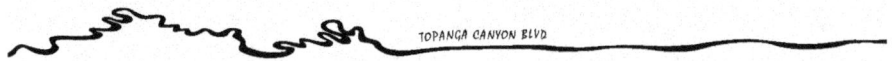

It was just a week later that I received an email from Kevin Grimes at Sunset Gower Productions about my script. He suggested we meet at The Ivy in Los Angeles to go over it. According to some quick research, that's where the movers and shakers of Hollywood met. I couldn't believe it. I was going to "take a meeting" with a Hollywood executive.

Lukas was excited for me. "Dude, what do you think he's going to say?" he exclaimed when he heard the news.

Visions of Emmy Awards and six figure contracts danced in my head. "I'm not sure," I said with restraint. "I don't want to get my hopes up. You shouldn't get your hopes up either." I needed to manage both of our expectations.

"Why would I get *my* hopes up?"

"You know—big money contract for me means big money stuff for you." Lukas liked it when I bought him "stuff."

"You think that little of me," he said, pouting. "I just want you to be successful."

"I know, I know." I was just giving him a hard time. I knew he had my best interests at heart.

When the morning of the meeting came, I was extremely nervous. What was Kevin going to say? Did he love my script? Did he hate it? Or would it be one of those middle-of-the-road reviews?

Lukas reminded me that I had nothing to lose and everything to gain. I'd pursued television writing on a whim. Even if it didn't work out, I was still an awesome teacher and I still had an awesome job that I loved. He even offered to come with me. I said he just probably wanted a free meal. "Damn right I do," he replied.

I was still feeling nervous when I pulled up to The Ivy on North Robertson. At least my black Audi looked sharp. "I'm here for a meeting," I told the valet.

"Yeah, you and everybody else," he sneered. He must have been a frustrated actor. I tossed him my keys in a miserable attempt at California cool. Lukas could have pulled it off. Maybe I *should* have invited him to come along.

As I entered, I looked across the room. Actors and producers, directors and writers were all engaged in deep conversation. I could only imagine the deals being made. I realized I wasn't at the Canyon Diner anymore, and felt extremely out of place. I was tempted to leave.

The maître d'—who was dressed in a tuxedo—finally acknowledged my presence. "I have a meeting with Kevin Grimes," I said. I expected to hear "Who?" as a response.

"Mr. Grimes, impressive," he murmured under his breath. "Mr. Grimes isn't here yet. But he is expecting you, Mr. Whitmore," he said smoothly. "Let me show you to his table." *Wow, he has a table*, I thought.

Grimes' table was definitely in a "see and be seen" location. I had expected to wait more privately in the lobby, maybe with one of those Applebee's pagers. I started sweating profusely, so much so that drops of sweat landed on the table. I assumed that the other patrons walking past Grimes' table were all staring at the sweaty man sitting alone. That made me even more uncomfortable. I was hoping I'd cool down by the time Mr. Grimes arrived, but I was also tempted to get up and leave.

I slowly sipped the glass of water on the table, centering myself. I focused on why I was there—to get feedback on my writing—and remembered what Lukas told me. I had nothing to lose and everything to gain.

The waiter brought Italian bread and a small dish of oil as an appetizer. He assured me that Mr. Grimes was on his way. I kept sipping the water, and finally stopped sweating. I tried to look important by continually checking my phone for messages that never appeared.

"Noah Whitmore?" a voice asked. I looked up to see a handsomely-dressed man about my age standing before me.

"Yes. Kevin Grimes?" I asked.

He nodded and put his briefcase down on the banquette, sitting down next to me. "Thank you for meeting me," he said, his demeanor was pleasant. I felt much more relaxed.

"How do you know my dad?" I asked.

"He didn't tell you?" Kevin seemed surprised.

I laughed. "My dad knows everyone. What did he do, arrest you?"

The minute I said it, I regretted it. I had probably blown the meeting with my sarcasm.

"Actually, he did," Kevin said nonchalantly. "When I was 17. For drug possession. Twice."

Well, that was surprising. Kevin went on to explain that my dad had seen potential in him, and, as a result, had offered to serve as his mentor. If it weren't for my dad, Kevin said, he'd be in jail, not making a living as a successful television executive.

"See, you never know where life will take you," I said. *Ain't that the truth*, I added to myself.

"Tell me about yourself," Kevin continued. "How'd you get interested in writing?"

It was time for me to share my story. I explained that I was a physics teacher at Malibu High, but part of me had always dreamed of a career in television. A colleague suggested that, as a teacher, I had a lot of stories to tell, and those stories would make for compelling television viewing.

"Well, that was your first mistake," Kevin said. I was surprised, but I figured Hollywood executives needed to be direct. They didn't have the time to waste.

"People always say that," he continued. "The truth is, while you might think your stories are interesting, the general public might not. At any rate, how did you develop this story?"

"I just tried to come up with realistic teacher situations."

"What's your connection to the characters?"

I thought for a minute. "Well, I combined some of the traits of some of my students and my colleagues," was the best I could come up with. He pounced on that.

"That's your second mistake. If you don't love your characters, then you'll find they are a chore to write for. If you love them, writing for them is easy."

That made sense. That might be why I struggled to finish the damn thing. "Overall, what did you think?" I said, cutting to the chase.

"Can I be honest with you?" Kevin asked in reply. I knew what was coming, and nodded, bracing myself.

"Your structure is off. Your characters talk way too much. Nothing seems to actually happen to your characters. There's no internal conflict. Your formatting needs improvement. You need a stronger story engine." As he rattled this off, Kevin showed me the script he had reviewed, now heavily annotated. There was more red ink than actual type. Now I knew how my students felt when they got back a paper covered with negative comments.

"Yikes," is all I could say in response.

"I'll be blunt," Kevin continued. "This really needs a lot of work."

"Is that the Hollywood way of saying 'it stinks'?"

Kevin smiled tightly. "Yes, it stinks."

I groaned. Now I had nothing to gain and everything to lose.

Kevin hadn't finished, though. "Not all is lost," he said. "You have a nugget of a good idea here. You need to make it unique."

All is not lost, I thought. I still struggled to reconcile this with all the criticism I'd just received.

"What would you tell your students?" Kevin added, watching me consider all this. "Just pack up and go home?"

"I'd never tell them that," I said. Maybe I'd said it to myself once or twice, though.

"Then don't tell yourself that either," he said. It sounded like the same advice I always gave my students—and Lukas.

Kevin suggested I take a class on scriptwriting to give me a better sense of script structure and dialogue. It seemed like a reasonable suggestion.

"You also need to find stories that are meaningful to you but global in theme," he said. "You want the viewer to root for your characters. You want your viewers to relate to your stories."

Maybe this review wasn't as bad as it initially seemed. "Any other advice?" I asked.

"Sure. When you have a solid rewrite, let me read it. Your dad has my contact information." That was a nice offer, considering.

With that, he tossed a $50 bill on the table, shook my hand and left. We hadn't even ordered food. I guess that's how Hollywood works.

I took a final sip of water and exited the restaurant. I was surprised to see Lukas leaning against to the valet stand.

"What are you doing here?" I asked.

"I came to see how things went," he said. That was sweet of him.

"How'd you get here?" I asked. I knew he hadn't skateboarded all the way from Topanga.

"Uber."

Two young girls approached us. "Could we have your autograph?" one asked shyly. I knew they didn't mean me.

Lukas took the 8 x 11 photograph she handed him and signed it "Timothée Chalamet." The girls squealed in delight and ran off.

"I'm not even going to ask," I said.

Lukas laughed. It felt like the old Lukas was back.

"So, how did it go?" he asked.

I rolled my eyes. "I don't see any Emmy awards in my near future."

"Was it that bad?" Lukas wanted to be supportive. His surprise visit was all the support I needed, though.

"Actually, no," I said. "He suggested I take a class or two. Find myself as a writer. Find my characters."

Lukas pointed to himself. "You got a character right here," he said. He was right about that.

"You're not giving up, are you?" he added. Lukas championed my dreams in the same way I always championed his.

"I don't know," I said, sighing. "Maybe I should just stay focused on my teaching."

Lukas hit me on the side of my head. "I want your greatest accomplishment to be making me proud of you," he said, smiling.

I hoped I already had.

NINE

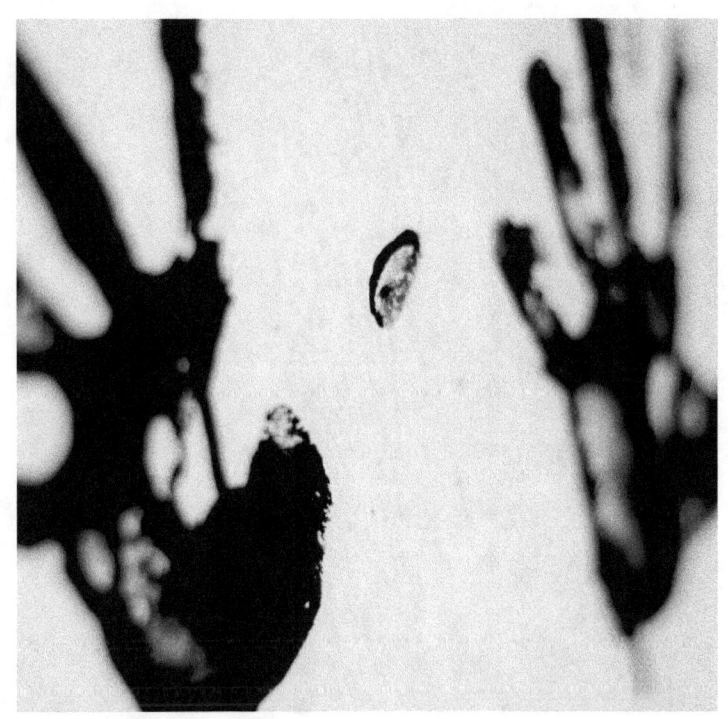

My meeting with Kevin Grimes and Lukas' faith in me gave me enough motivation to head to the UCLA Extension office on Gayley. Even after all these years, there was something intoxicating about stepping onto the UCLA Campus. A flood of memories came over me as I did. I had enjoyed my time there immensely.

A young man named Jeff stood at the counter as I entered the office. "May I help you, sir?" he asked.

He called me sir. I was officially old. Ignoring that for now, I explained to Jeff that I was interested in taking a television writing course. I also told him I was an alum: class of... many years ago.

"Most of our summer courses have already started or are full. Let me see what's available," he said, clacking away on the computer. "Well, sir. We've got two courses left for you. One is Introduction to Dialogue Writing. That's an online course. It started yesterday. Then we have Flash Fiction. It meets Wednesday and Friday mornings, 9 to 11. First class is tomorrow with Dr. Francis." Jeff assured me he was an excellent professor.

I thought for a minute. Dialogue writing seemed like the safest choice. I could take it from the comfort of my own home. I wouldn't have to interact with any other aspiring writers. This would work well with my introverted personality. But Flash Fiction would force me to put myself—and my aspirations of being any semblance of a writer—out into the open.

"What is flash fiction?" I asked.

In response, Jeff clacked away on his computer again. I would have thought he'd know off the top of his head.

"'Learn to write prose of 500-1000 words in this workshop focused on condensing story down to its most essential and memorable parts,'" he read from the course description.

It sounded like short story writing. I thought I might be able to do that.

"Sign me up for Flash Fiction," I said. Another decision that would change my life.

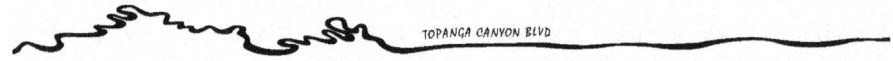

TOPANGA CANYON BLVD

It was the end of another day at summer camp. Every summer, the maintenance staff at Malibu High started preparing for the new school year. Emery had told Lukas that always meant the maintenance men threw away a lot of interesting stuff. It was school tradition for teachers and students to snoop around the trash piles. Emery once found a fully-functional

Palm Pilot, which he had sold on eBay for a hefty profit. Knowing his luck, Lukas was pretty sure he'd only find a box of pencils.

When drop-off was finished, Lukas headed down to the dumpsters to see what was available. No one else was around. He found broken desks, discarded boxes of paper clips, and some ancient calendars. Disappointed, Lukas was just about to head back to work when something intriguing caught his eye. It was an acoustic guitar. It looked brand new.

Lukas scooped up the guitar and slung it over his back. He felt like he was stealing it. Grabbing a marker from the dumpster, he wrote his name on the back. Now it was officially his. He walked back to the circle, where I pulled up just as he arrived at the curb. He tossed his backpack in the back seat, along with the guitar.

"Where'd you get the guitar?" I asked. I knew he hadn't left with it in the morning.

"It's cleaning day. I found it in the trash." Lukas seemed pleased he had scored a quality piece of merchandise.

"Are you sure you found it in the trash?" I asked. I hoped he hadn't made a five-finger discount in the music department.

"What do you think I did? Steal it?" Lukas seemed offended. "I used to play guitar a little when I lived in Miami," he added. I had no idea he had any interest in guitar.

We headed to the Canyon Diner for dinner. Lukas was proud of his find and decided to bring it in with him. Olivia looked surprised. "I didn't know you were performing tonight!" she exclaimed.

Lukas had no idea what she was talking about. "What do you mean? Performing?"

"It's open mic night in the bar," she said. "You are a little young. But cute and talented might take you far."

As she spoke, Olivia showed us to our table. She didn't even bother giving us menus. We never ordered anything different.

"Nah, I'm not performing," Lukas said. "I found the guitar in the trash at school. I used to play back in Florida."

"Well, if you're ever interested in playing here, let me know," she replied. "Next open mic night is in two weeks." Lukas smiled as she headed off to put in our order.

"Do you want do it?" I asked.

"Do what?" Lukas seemed confused.

"Play a song for their open mic night?" I egged him on, not knowing yet how it would rebound back on me.

"You can't be serious."

"Why not?" I asked. "You were the one who told *me* to try something new."

Lukas never liked it when his own words came back to bite him in the butt. "Why don't *you* get up there and do a reading or something?" he countered. He knew I probably didn't have the guts to do that either.

"Maybe I just will," I said. I was bluffing. I got nervous meeting a Hollywood executive. There's no way I'd get up on a stage and perform.

"You won't. You'll chicken out at the last minute," Lukas taunted. He knew me very well.

"I'll put my cards on the table if you will," I retorted, laying down the marker.

"Wait, we're playing cards now?" Lukas asked, bewildered. He never understood my metaphors.

I smiled. "I'll keep it simple. Just for you." Just then, Olivia arrived with our food. Lukas threw a roll in my direction.

"Boys, boys," she said. "Act your age. Somewhat."

"We're having a little discussion about the open mic night in two weeks," I said.

Olivia got excited and turned to Lukas. "You're gonna do it?"

"He wants me to," he said, pointing at me. "I want *him* to."

"Why don't you both perform?" Olivia suggested. "There's a $100 prize for first place."

"Let's make a deal!" Lukas said. "Winner buys the other dinner."

"I don't know, boys—don't be so sure of yourselves," Olivia teased us. "Competition at the Canyon Diner Open Mic Night is pretty stiff."

"Let's try this," I suggested. "Whatever the outcome, Olivia picks the best of the two of us. Loser buys the winner dinner."

"See, you're already a poet," Lukas said, laughing. I flung the roll back in his direction before we shook hands. It was game on.

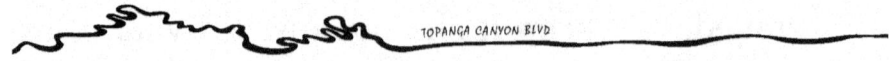

The two weeks between the bet and Open Mic Night passed quickly. I used my time in my Flash

Fiction class to try to perfect a short piece. Dr. Francis seemed agitated that I was trying to make one of his assignments into a performance piece. I knew how much I hated it when my students went off-topic with an assignment. In any case, I found I was getting nowhere, and put it aside to use my class time to work on original pieces.

Meanwhile, Lukas was using all of his free time at work to try to compose a song. He even tried the advice that Kevin Grimes had given me: write about things that are meaningful. That advice didn't seem to help him either. His mind wandered during the song-writing process, and he found each subsequent version to be worse than the previous one.

The day before Open Mic Night, Lukas was out on some adventure with Emery and told me he would be home late. I used this time to work on my performance, staring down at the blank yellow legal pad before me. I tried writing about school and about Lukas and about Topanga. Nothing seemed to flow and nothing seemed to work. I finally tossed the legal pad aside and turned on the TV for inspiration.

Lukas had left an episode of *Silver Spoons* paused on Hulu. It was the one where Edward Stratton had to run up the stairs of the Empire State Building for a fundraiser. Boy, did he have determination and stamina. I had neither. I thought I might just concede the competition to Lukas. Eager to take a break, I hit restart, and the episode started anew.

As the episode progressed, a light bulb came on in my mind. I picked up my legal pad again and scribbled on it furiously. When I had finished, I ripped out the piece of paper with my work on it and headed upstairs to bed. I knew I had the winning performance.

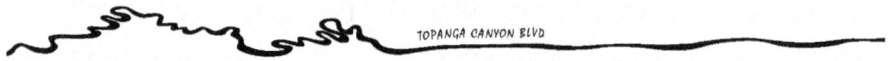

TOPANGA CANYON BLVD

Lukas arrived home shortly after 11 PM. Open Mic Night was tomorrow, and he still had no song. He was sure that I had written a winning poem or story, while his music sheets were blank.

He picked up his guitar and started strumming quietly so as to not wake me. He tried a number of themes—his mother, California, Miami, Emery, the beach, the Top of Topanga. No matter what he wrote, though, Lukas soon discovered it stunk. *Maybe I should just concede the competition*, he thought. He finally tossed his Hal Leonard Music Notebook aside and turned on the TV for inspiration.

Lukas noticed that I had left the *Races with Eagles* episode of *Silver Spoons* paused, and hit restart. As the episode progressed, a light bulb came on in his head. He grabbed his music notebook and started scribbling furiously. After a minute or two, he finished his writing and smiled to himself. He picked up his notebook and guitar and headed upstairs to bed. He knew he had the winning performance.

Open Mic Night was finally here. As the hour to leave approached, Lukas was sitting in the living room, watching yet another rerun of *Silver Spoons*.

"What are you watching?" I asked. I'm not sure why I asked every time. Lately, the answer was always the same.

"*Silver Spoons*. It's the one where Rick becomes a peer counselor," he said. That seemed to be a required "very special episode" for every 1980s sitcom.

I looked him over. "Is that what you're wearing?" I asked. Lukas had on his usual khaki shorts, Malibu soccer T-shirt, black Converse sneakers, and no socks. There were spaghetti stains on the T-shirt. I thought he might have gotten a *little* more dressed up for his performance.

"It's open mic night. You're supposed to look hip. Not like Felix Unger." Since living with me, Lukas's sitcom knowledge had expanded all the way back to the 1970s.

"What's wrong with what I'm wearing?" I asked defensively. I wore a clean, plaid short-sleeve shirt, khaki pants and black shoes. I realized I looked like I had stepped out of an episode of *Father Knows Best*. If this was a fashion competition, I was doomed to fail.

Lukas grabbed his guitar and his music notebook and headed to the front door. "Ready to lose, old man?" he called out over his shoulder. I grabbed my writer's notebook and followed him out the door. *No,* I thought, *I'm ready to win.*

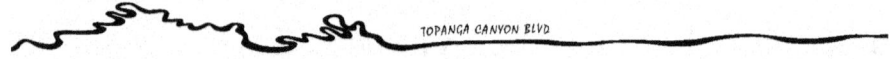
TOPANGA CANYON BLVD

The parking lot of the Canyon Diner was filled when we arrived. Olivia was right: Open Mic Night was a huge draw.

Pat, my dad, and Emery were seated at a small table in the back corner. I believe this was the first time I'd actually ever been inside the Canyon Diner's dining room. I'd always eaten outside on the patio.

Lukas and I surveyed the room and saw a number of people with threadbare journals and musical instruments.

"Lot of competition here," I observed.

"Not for squarest outfit," Lukas commented wryly. I should have changed before I left.

We sat down at the table and greeted our friends.

"You guys nervous?" Emery asked.

Lukas tapped his musical notebook before strumming his guitar. "Got a winner right here," he declared.

"Says you," I replied. I tapped my journal. "The winner's in here."

As we were bantering, Olivia took the stage to open the program. She noted that the competition was pretty heated tonight, and then announced the first act.

The first few acts were all unique. One aspiring opera singer performed a rap version of *Habanera*; another contestant did an interpretive dance to Steve Winwood's *Higher Love*. All of the performers that preceded us were quite good. I felt a little nervous.

After an hour, we reached the intermission. Olivia came over to our table and informed us that Lukas would be up next, followed by me.

"Good luck," Pat said. "You're both winners!"

As the program resumed, Olivia introduced Lukas as "an aspiring songwriter from Topanga, by way of Miami." Lukas grabbed his guitar and his music and walked up to the stage. I watched him go with pride. Regardless of our competition, I wanted Lukas to perform well. While he tuned the guitar, Emery yelled out, "Chalamet!"

Lukas strummed his guitar a few times before introducing himself to the crowd. "Hey dudes and dudettes. Call me Lukas. I'm here to do a little song I think you'll like," he said.

"My song doesn't require any introduction. After all," he added, "good music speaks for itself." I took a quick picture of him on stage as he spoke.

Lukas coughed a few times and warbled:

"Here we are, face to face
A couple of silver spoons.
Hopin' to find, we're two of a kind
Making a go, making it grow.
Together, we're going to find our way.
Together, taking the time each day.

To learn all about those things you just can't buy.
Two silver spoons together.
You and I together. We're going to find our way.
You and I together. We're going to find our way.
You and I together."

I gulped. Lukas had performed the theme song to *Silver Spoons*. Not even an original song. He could play the guitar but he sure couldn't sing. In spite of this, Pat applauded wildly. Emery had a shocked look on his face and my dad looked confused. The crowd gave him tepid applause. Lukas bowed in recognition and returned to the table.

"Nice job," I commented dryly. "All you did was sing a TV theme song."

"You told me to perform something meaningful, right?" he fired back. I couldn't argue with that, and he smirked at my silence. "Let's hear what you got, dude," he said.

I looked down at my journal. "I think I'm gonna pass," I said.

Lukas laughed. "I knew it. I knew you were going to cop out."

I didn't want to drop out. But I also knew what I'd written in my notebook.

It was too late to call it off anyway. Olivia was calling me up on stage, introducing me as "a high school physics teacher and a fish & chips lover." She assured the crowd they wouldn't be disappointed in my performance as I was "a talented writer too." She could not have been more wrong.

I took to the stage and smiled. Lukas snapped a picture of me. Sitting down on the stool, I leaned into the microphone and started my reading.

"Here we are, face to face
A couple of silver spoons.
Hopin' to find, we're two of a kind
Making a go, making it grow.
Together, we're going to find our way.
Together, taking the time each day.
To learn all about those things you just can't buy.
Two silver spoons together.
You and I together. We're going to find our way.
You and I together. We're going to find our way.
You and I together."

Lukas stood up and screamed, "Foul! You can't perform the same thing I as me."

I turned to the crowd and said, "Pure coincidence." They gave me a tepid round of applause as well. At least they didn't boo.

I returned to the table and Lukas just stared at me, aghast. "Dude, where'd you get that idea from?" he asked.

I had to be honest. "You left that repeat on pause. I'd run out of ideas. What about you?"

Lukas laughed. "I found the same repeat. Plus, the rules didn't say you had to have original material."

He was right about that. Olivia made her way over to our table as the last act performed.

"Who's the winner?" Lukas asked.

She smiled. "You are both winners. I declare a tie." It was the only fair result. Olivia promised to bring us a pitcher of soda, on the house.

Dad was still confused. "What was that all about?" he asked. Pat sought to clear it up, but her psychoanalytical explanation fell flat.

"Your friend Grimes told me to write from the heart," I said to Dad. As corny as it might be, I felt those few words best represented the relationship that Lukas and I had.

Lukas fidgeted in his seat. "I'm not sure we're silver spoons," he admitted.

"But it's you and I together," I reminded him.

TEN

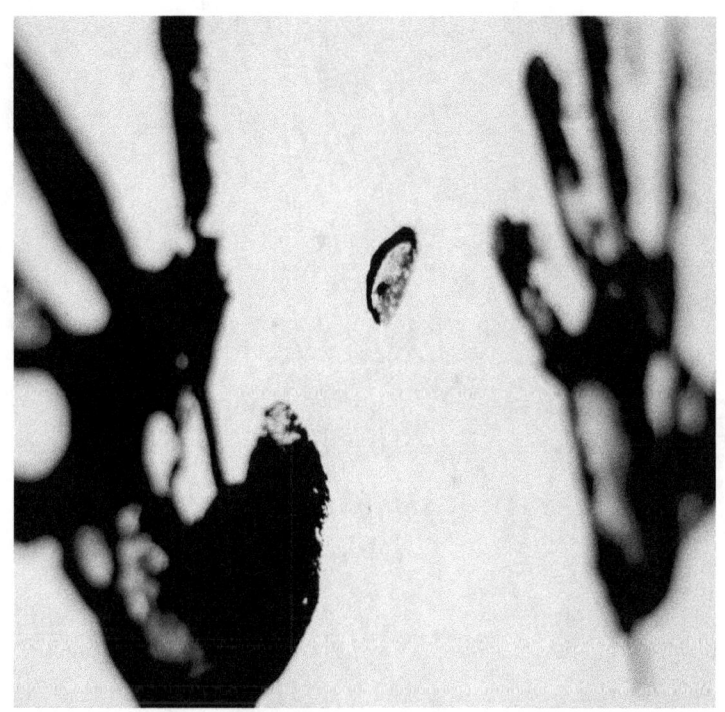

The summer was quickly coming to a close. It had been a whirlwind, and I was frustrated that I hadn't prepared at all for the new school year. With Lukas in my orbit, though, my summer had been filled with positive new experiences. I knew that I'd have to start thinking about what to do with him for the upcoming school year. He had settled into a comfortable life here in Topanga, and I didn't want to see that upended. He'd also given my life more meaning and purpose.

My thoughts were interrupted by my phone ringing. The call was from Kate Seibold, a college classmate and former girlfriend whom I'd remained friends with over the years. While I had gone off to a career in education, she had pursued a career in marketing. She currently worked at Paramount, focusing on emerging media and new productions. We'd have lunch once a year to catch up. I loved driving onto the Paramount lot and

telling the guard, "I'm here for a meeting." This may have been the genesis of my interest in writing.

"Is it time for our annual lunch already?" I asked Kate.

"No. More of an opportunity. Would you be interested in a ticket to a taping?"

"What show?"

"It's a pilot called *Up for Anything*. New Disney Channel show."

"That sounds like fun. Could I get two tickets?"

"Two? Is there something you're not telling me?" Kate liked prying into my personal life whenever she could.

"It's rather complicated," I replied. "I'll explain when I see you." Lukas required an in-person explanation.

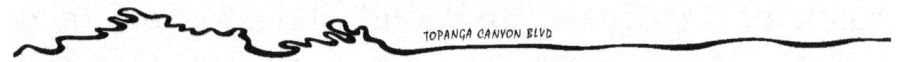

As we drove from Topanga to Paramount, Lukas assumed his usual pretzel shape in the front seat of the Audi.

"Couldn't you have at least dressed up for this?" I asked, eyeing his clothes with disdain.

"I am dressed up," he replied, pointing to his feet. "I wore socks."

I had to laugh. He could be the star of his own television show.

"What's this show about anyway?" Lukas asked.

"Like every other Disney Channel show. Some suburban family with a bunch of wiseass kids."

"Not exactly *Silver Spoons*."

"That show just had a wiseass dad and son," I said. "Same thing."

We drove onto the lot, and I explained to the guard that we were there to meet Kate Seibold. The guard looked at his list, checked off our names, passed us two official Paramount Studios nametags and directed us to park in the lot near the blue-sky tank. Kate would meet us at the sound stage.

Once we parked, Lukas got out of the car and looked around. "Now this is pretty cool," he said. He did have a curious nature about him.

"Which sound stage do we go to?" he added.

I looked down at my phone. "25."

We looked at the map. "It's up that-a-way," Lukas pointed out. Then he paused. "Do you think we'd get in trouble if we sort of walked around first? Maybe we'll see someone famous!" he exclaimed. I shrugged. With our luck, we'd probably meet Adam Sandler's brother.

Lukas was clearly intrigued by the atmosphere of a studio lot. I tried to explain to him why it was called a lot, but he wasn't that curious. "I'm not sure where

25 is," I said finally. "What if we take the more scenic tour to get there?" That worked for him.

We headed down Avenue J and then walked through the New York backlot. "This looks just like New York City," he said.

"You've been to New York?" I asked, surprised.

"No. But this looks like New York." Lukas poked around some of the doorways and walked into the corner café that had appeared in a number of TV shows. After he had satisfied his curiosity about the New York backlot, we asked one of the production crew to take a picture of us in front of the *Mission: Impossible* office building.

We circled around the back of the lot to Leonard Nimoy Way. Still eager to explore, Lukas approached the door to Stage 30. He didn't notice the red light outside the door, and even if he had, I'm not sure he knew what it meant: that a show was taping inside. In other words, DO NOT DISTURB. Before I had a chance to warn him, Lukas opened the door to the sound stage, and an alarm shrieked. He was immediately almost tackled by two security guards. An important-looking studio executive followed the guards out the door.

"What's wrong with you?" she yelled.

Lukas only stuttered for a response. He slowly backed away from the door and returned to my side. "Well, I won't do that again," he said in his own defense.

Lukas asked if he could go look at some of the plaques on another nearby studio. He promised not to open any doors.

I turned to see one of the studio tour golf carts approaching. It stopped near me and about six giggly teenage girls got off. The tour guide was explaining how Dr. Phil had filmed a show on one of the soundstages earlier in the day. Now was the perfect time for my temporary tattoo payback.

The girls were snapping photos of the soundstage doors and of anything that looked Instagram-worthy. I approached the tour guide, flashed my official ID, and asked if she thought the girls on the tour would be interested in seeing a celebrity. The tour guide whirled her head around, looking for a celebrity. "Where?" she asked.

I pointed in Lukas' direction and simply stated, "Timothée Chalamet."

A collective shriek went up from the girls, and in record time, the small gaggle nearly assaulted Lukas. I'd never see so many selfies taken in such a short period of time. One girl shoved an autograph book in his direction. Another almost pulled out a lock of Lukas' hair. I held my phone up and recorded the whole incident. I'd have posted it on Instagram if I actually had an account.

The faux celebrity encounter lasted almost five minutes before the tour guide managed to get the girls away from Lukas. He stumbled in my direction.

"What was that?" he asked.

I started laughing and he scowled. "You think it's funny?" he asked, whacking me in the arm.

"The look on your face was priceless," I said, showing him the video on my phone.

"You better be careful," he warned me. "Payback can be a bitch." Lukas was very good at payback—I'd give him credit for that.

I looked at my watch. "We better get going," I said. I hated being late.

We arrived at Soundstage 25 without further incident. A long line of people, mostly tweens and their parents, were waiting for the taping. We flashed our IDs and were escorted to the VIP line. Kate found me there. She did a double take when she saw Lukas with me.

"This is Lukas," I said by way of introduction. Kate extended her hand.

"Something you haven't told me?" Kate asked, a quizzical look her face. "Surprise son?" *Hmmm, that could be a TV show*, I thought.

"Lukas is my cousin. He's been living with me," I said.

Kate gave him a long look. "Did anyone ever tell you that you look like..."

"Yeah, I get that a lot," Lukas said. "As a matter of fact, I just got it." He rubbed his shoulder as he spoke. One of the giddy teenage girls had almost dislocated it.

Kate escorted us past the line of enthusiastic tweens and their parents and into the studio. She had reserved front row seats for us. As we settled in, the other attendees slowly filled into the studio, chattering nonstop.

The set met every requirement of a typical Disney Channel show, featuring a standard suburban living room and kitchen, a high school classroom and hallway, and a teenager's bedroom. Kate explained the premise of the show to us: a teenage girl becomes popular on social media when she creates a YouTube channel called *Up for Anything*, where she gets her friends and family to undertake a variety of stunts and tricks. It sounded lame. Lukas just rolled his eyes.

"I'll meet you back here after the show," Kate said. She left the bleachers and headed up to the stage, where a middle-aged comedian was introducing himself. His name was Shecky Clark. I got the feeling he was at the pinnacle of his career.

Shecky gave an overview of the show's premise before getting into his act. Lukas leaned over and asked me, "How long does this part go on for?" Apparently, Shecky had a lot of material. None of it was funny, but at least he didn't steal the theme to *Silver Spoons.*

It didn't take much to warm up the audience. Every time Shecky mentioned the name of one of the stars, the tweens screamed wildly. Lukas, in the meantime, was hanging his head back over the back of the chair.

Shecky still had one more bit to do before the show started filming, though. "Who would like to film a scene with the cast of *Up for Anything*?" he asked the crowd. He then introduced two of the stars, a teenage girl named Vanessa Jenkins and a teenage boy named Jackson Moreno. Apparently, all Disney

Channel stars were required to be cute with dimples. These two fit the bill. More shrieking followed.

"Do I have a volunteer?" Shecky asked. Even more shrieking. Every tween girl in the audience wanted a shot to be on stage with the flawlessly handsome Joshua. Shecky apparently had a hard time picking one for the opportunity. I pointed in Lukas' direction. He was the only boy in the audience.

I elbowed Lukas and whispered, "Shecky wants you." Lukas bolted upright in his seat. He had fallen asleep. Shecky saw Lukas' jolt as an expression of interest, and approached him with a microphone.

"What's your name, young man?" he asked

"Stranger danger," was all Lukas could say. The audience roared.

Shecky rolled his eyes. "Well, someone thinks he's funny," he announced to the crowd.

I whispered to Lukas, "Just go with it. Be up for anything."

Shecky pulled Lukas up onstage, and the audience murmured excitedly as they took him in. "The ladies seem to like you," Shecky noted.

Lukas didn't have any patience for any of it. He stood onstage with his hands deep in his pockets and shot me a dirty look before introducing himself as Lukas from Topanga.

"Did anyone ever tell you..." Shecky began.

"Yeah, yeah. Just move it along." Lukas was over it. It was funny to see him so uncomfortable.

Vanessa and Jackson shook Lukas' hand and Shecky gave him a copy of the script. The scene had Lukas' character, named Ryan, showing up unexpectedly for a date with Vanessa, while Joshua harbored a secret crush on Vanessa. It was straight out of *iCarly*.

At this point, Lukas was truly up for anything. He eventually dropped the script and just made up his own lines. That clearly frustrated Vanessa and Jackson, who weren't really "up for anything." They soon left the stage in disgust, with Jackson muttering, "What a jerk!"

Shecky did one of those "Let's hear it for Lukas" lines and gave him a one-size-fits-all *Up for Anything* T-shirt. He made his way back over to me as Shecky wrapped up.

"How'd you like that?" I asked him.

Lukas grinned. "It was fun actually."

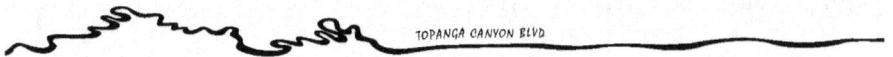

TOPANGA CANYON BLVD

The show taping wrapped by 7 PM. Kate told us she would meet us in the Paramount Studios Dining Room afterward.

As we headed to dinner, I asked Lukas what he thought of the show.

"I'm not sure I'm part of their target audience," he said diplomatically. Neither was I.

"It was a fun experience though," he continued. "I think you could write a better show. And I liked the acting thing."

We made our way down Avenue C. It should have been a short walk, but Lukas ricocheted from side to side, insisting on looking at every sign and soundstage we passed. When we arrived at the Dining Room, Kate was waiting for us.

"How'd you like the show?" she asked, clearly hoping for positive feedback. She wasn't going to get it from us.

"It was ok," Lukas announced, speaking for both of us.

"I heard you had fun in the audience participation part," she prompted him.

"Yeah, it was cool," he said. As we talked about the show, the maître d' seated us at a prime table. More movers and shakers all around us.

Lukas excused himself to go to the bathroom soon afterward, and Kate quickly turned to me, her curiosity building. "So. Lukas. Care to explain?" she asked.

I went over the short version of how Lukas had ended up in southern California, and how he had become my responsibility over the past eight months or so.

"I told you that you'd be a great dad," she said when I'd finished.

"Let's not get ahead of ourselves. Let's start with guardian."

"I've known you a long time.," Kate said, smiling. "I can see it in your eyes."

"See what?" I asked

"He's like a son to you, isn't he?" she said. I had to admit that was true.

Lukas soon returned from his bathroom trip and plopped down in the chair next to me. "Thanks for the tickets, Ms. Seibold," he said. "I really did have a great time."

The waiter interrupted our conversation to ask for our order, but Kate quickly said we needed more time. She was definitely a woman in control. I respected that about her. I think that's why we remained friends for so long.

Lukas pointed at me. "You know he's written a script for a TV show," he told Kate

"Really?" Kate responded, turning to me. "How many more secrets are you keeping from me?" she asked

"And he met with a big-time Hollywood person about it!" Lukas exclaimed. He had a big mouth.

Kate looked sad. "Why wouldn't you share it with me?"

I explained that I didn't want to use my friendship with her just to get ahead, and that the opportunity with Kevin Grimes had fallen into my lap. She understood. Or she said she did.

"What kind of response did you get?" she asked.

I repeated the line I used with Lukas: "I don't foresee any Emmy awards in my future." I added that Kevin Grimes suggested I find characters I love, not just characters to write about. Kate offered to read it too.

The conversation then switched back to Lukas and I. "What have you two been up to all summer?" she asked.

I pulled out my phone and showed Kate some photos: our trip to Santa Barbara, Lukas working at camp, me in the hospital. She seemed annoyed that I hadn't informed her of that last part.

"I'm also taking a flash fiction course at UCLA," I added.

"And how do you like that?"

"I've really enjoyed it. I like the short form of it. I've also gotten a lot of positive feedback on my writing." In fact, I liked the course so much, I had already signed up for Flash Fiction 2 in the fall.

The waiter soon returned to take our order. Lukas quickly perused the menu and pointed to the spaghetti and meatballs. Even though Kate was treating, I resisted the temptation to order the most expensive thing on the menu, and settled on the mac and cheese with truffles. Kate went with the Cobb Salad.

Lukas then turned inquisitor and started asking Kate about her job, about studio policies and procedures, about what shows were filming there. I smiled to see how maturely he could handle himself— at times. Kate was impressed as well, and graciously answered all of his questions.

Lukas wanted to know if there were other TV show tapings he could attend. "I'll tell you what," Kate said. "Before you head back to school, I'll make arrangements for you to have a private tour of the studios."

"Really? That'd be awesome," he said, slouching down in his chair.

"Sit up straight," I told him. Kate smiled.

Our food soon arrived and we spent a few minutes in silence eating. I looked over at Kate, who had what one might call her thinking face on. She would have the same look on her face in college, whenever we had to come up with an idea for a group project.

"I know that look. You're cooking up some crazy idea," I said.

"I'm just putting two and two together," she said innocently.

"Did you come up with four?" I was pretty quick with math and science.

"You said Kevin Grimes told you to write about characters you love," she began.

"He sure did," Lukas chimed in.

"And?" I asked

"You have one right here," Kate said. I looked at Lukas, who slurped his spaghetti so hard that not only did the whole restaurant hear him, but his face and shirt were immediately splattered with sauce. I couldn't resist taking a picture.

"What do you mean?" I asked, turning back to Kate.

"Listen to me carefully. You have a lot of pictures that tell a compelling story," she said, pointing to my phone. "And you seem to have found a niche in writing short stories."

"I do like that," I admitted.

"He sure does." Lukas chimed in again.

"So why not take those pictures, write the stories of those pictures and then publish a book?"

"How does that get me success as a television writer?" I countered.

"Yeah, how does it?" Lukas kept chiming in.

"Thirteen stories. One book. Thirteen episodes. One season. There's a huge need for new programming these days," she said authoritatively. "Use your book as an idea for a series."

Kate knew the ins and outs of television production, and was always quick to propose intriguing ideas. I liked this one. "But what do I know about publishing a book?" I said. It was even less than what I knew about promoting a TV series script.

"Self-publishing is easy," Kate said. "A number of my colleagues have done it. I can connect you with one of them—if you will let me."

This seemed like something I could be successful at that did not involve teaching. I liked this idea more and more.

I looked over at Lukas. "What do you think?" I asked.

Lukas laughed. "It's not for me to decide. But even if it never makes it to air, you'd still be a published author."

Lukas always had faith in me. And I found that I had renewed faith in myself.

As we left the Paramount Studios and headed back to Topanga, Lukas could not stop talking about his experience at the studio. Even though he hated the show, he liked the idea of being on stage. Maybe a career in acting was in his future.

Meanwhile, my mind was churning with story ideas. I certainly had a lot of stories I could tell about Lukas and about being a teacher. I thought back to the advice Kevin Grimes gave me: write about characters you love. I looked over at Lukas, who had stopped talking and was just staring out the window.

I just need a title, I thought. My Flash Fiction course had taught me that by starting with a title, a writer forced the action to follow.

The traffic slowed considerably as we approached exit 27B on the 101, and soon came to a dead stop. "This is going to take forever," Lukas complained.

As we sat there together, I looked up at the green exit sign overhead, and found my title. *My Life with Lukas On Topanga Canyon Boulevard.*

ELEVEN

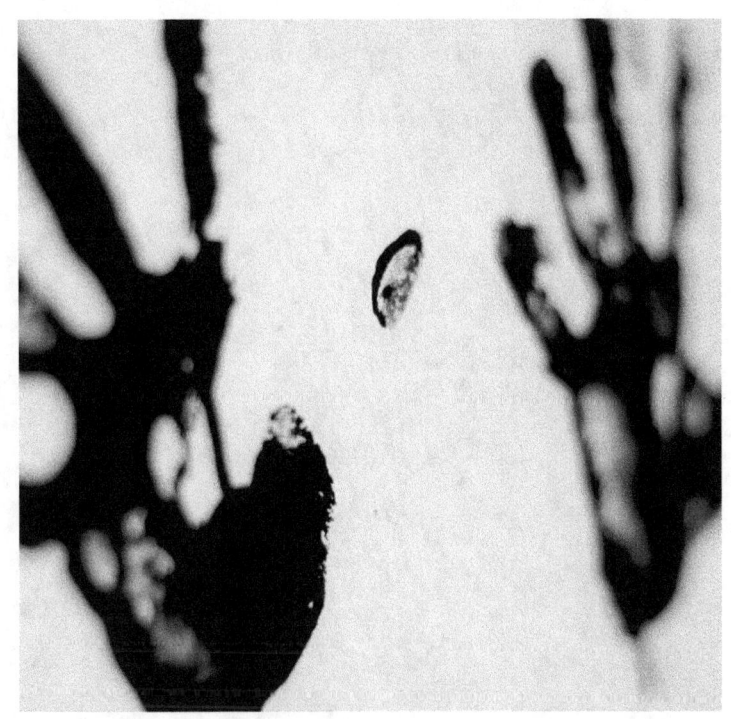

The summer was quickly coming to an end.

My last Flash Fiction class met the week after our visit to Paramount Studios. I had completed all of my work in a timely manner, and Dr. Francis especially liked my final piece, a fantasy story in which Lukas becomes a school principal. His comments were no different that the comments I received on my previous pieces. *Be more descriptive with your characters and your locations. Don't assume that the reader knows!* It was par for the course of being an aspiring writer.

We sat in his cluttered office in the basement of Ackerman. The book shelves were loaded up with classics and new releases. His desk was covered with ungraded papers, department memos, and newspaper clippings. If Lukas ever had an office, I imagined his office would look much like this.

"How do you feel the course went?" Dr. Francis asked me. As a teacher, I was familiar with that question: the indirect course evaluation. Student responses could be ego-boosting or ego-crushing.

"I had a pretty rough start. My work was awful," I admitted. "The rewrites and the feedback helped me a lot."

"The greatest joy of being a writer is having the opportunity to tell stories," Dr. Francis reminded me. "You've worked hard to improve your writing over the course of the summer."

"I'm pretty sure I'm not going to win a Pulitzer of an Emmy," I replied, although everyone in my small circle of friends and family seemed to think so.

"I did notice a consistent theme in all of your writing," Dr. Francis said, flipping through a pile of papers trying to find one of my assignments. It took him a while.

Here it comes, I thought, before asking "And what theme was that?"

"You seem to focus on the marginalized. You like to write about this Lukas character, who seems on the fringes of many of his experiences. Is Lukas a real person, a compilation of people, or you as a child?"

The question threw me for a minute. I realized that while the stories were about Lukas, they could have also been about me. Our lives' journeys were remarkably parallel.

I didn't feel like giving Dr. Francis a full explanation. "My writing is about a person who is very important to me," I said. That's all I felt like sharing.

Dr. Francis smiled. I think he thought I was talking about a significant other.

"I do have a question for you," I continued. I shared Kate's suggestion about self-publishing my work. He laughed.

"I'm serious."

"I know," he said. "I get that question a lot."

"And do you have an answer?"

"I do. Don't," he said. At least he was direct. I frowned in disappointment.

"But your enthusiasm for your character jumps off the page at me," he added. "I can tell that you care about your character."

Lukas was a character, all right. And I did care deeply for him. I nodded in agreement.

"If you choose to pursue this, I have two pieces of advice for you," he said as we wrapped up. "Keep writing from the heart. And find an excellent editor."

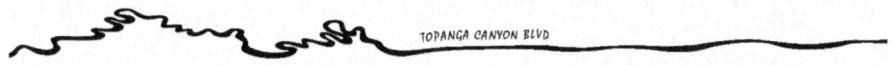

The final day of summer soccer camp had arrived. Lukas spied little Liam sitting on the picnic table bench, all alone. It brought Lukas back to the beginning of the summer. It also reminded him of his own youth.

Lukas sat down on the bench next to him. "What's up, little dude?" he asked. "Why are you all alone?"

"I'm sad," Liam announced.

"And why are you sad?"

"Because it's the end of camp. That makes me sad."

"And why does that make you sad?"

"Because I have to say goodbye to all of my friends," the boy sniffled. "And to you."

Lukas was tempted to give him a hug. "I'll still be your friend," he said.

Liam smiled. "Will you still teach me soccer?"

Lukas was surprised. The kid actually like soccer now. Now Lukas understood how I felt helping a troubled student. Or a troubled teenager, like Lukas.

"If you want me to, I will," he promised Liam. "You gonna keep practicing?"

"Every day, dude. Every day."

Lukas smiled to hear Liam adopting his lingo. He extended his hand and Liam shook it. "Make me proud, little dude," he said. "Make me proud."

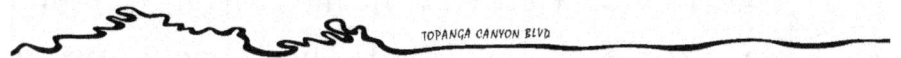

I got here as fast as I could," Pat said, sitting down next to me. We were out on the deck of Malibu Coffee + Tea.

"It wasn't an emergency. I just needed some friendly advice," I said, taking a sip of my coffee.

"What's up?" Pat asked. She was being a friend at this point, not a psychologist.

"I've gotten a call from Lukas' dad," I told her. "In short, he wants Lukas to return to Miami."

Pat's concern was genuine as she took this in. "I wasn't expecting that. What did you say to him?"

"I wasn't quite sure what to say," I told Pat. I'd become so accustomed to having Lukas as part of my life. I couldn't imagine not having a life with Lukas on Topanga Canyon Boulevard.

"I think your heart knows what to do," Pat said. She was right. My heart knew.

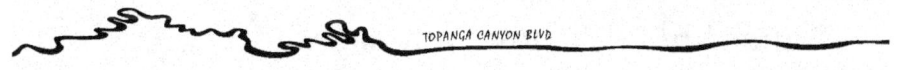

Emery and Lukas finished their clean-up details. With everything stored away for the season, summer camp was now officially closed. They headed out to Emery's Mercedes in the parking lot.

"Take the long way back to my house. I need some Top of Topanga time," Lukas said, pretzel-shaping himself in the front seat. He stared out the window as Emery took off.

The PCH was packed with traffic for a Friday afternoon, so Emery took the backroads through the mountains. The Top of Topanga was deserted when they arrived. Lukas got out of the car and hopped up onto the back of his favorite bench. He looked rather glum.

"Why are you sad, buddy?" Emery asked.

Lukas felt like he'd just had the same conversation with Liam an hour before. "Because the summer's over," he said.

"Don't wanna go back to school?"

"I'm not sure I wanna go back to school in Miami." Lukas took out his phone and played the voicemail his dad had left earlier in the day, by way of explanation.

"Whoa, dude. So now your dad wants you to come back to Miami?"

"Apparently."

Emery didn't want his friend to leave. "What are you going to do?" he asked.

Lukas sighed. "I've given Noah nothing but grief since I've been here. He's been nothing but awesome in return. He's been like a dad to me." Lukas hesitated for a minute before continuing. "And you've been the best bud anyone could ask for."

"Aww," Emery said. "You really want to stay, don't you?"

"If you'd asked me eight months ago, I'd have told you I didn't want to be here at all. Now I can't imagine being anywhere else."

"I think your heart knows what to do," Emery said. He was right. Lukas' heart knew.

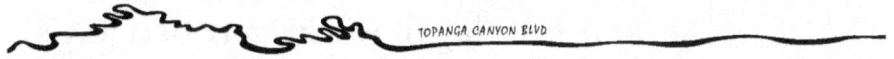
TOPANGA CANYON BLVD

I sat on the sofa at home, nursing a midnight mocha iced coffee. My dad sipped a cup of hot coffee.

"Lukas' dad wants him back?" Dad asked.

"That's what he said."

"Do you think Lukas has talked to his dad yet?" Even if he didn't say it, my dad knew I'd grown accustomed to having Lukas around.

I didn't know what Lukas had heard. I just knew I'd miss him if he went back to Miami. The summer had seemed like a big tailspin for both of us. But I wouldn't trade that chaos for anything.

We heard some light crunching from outside and knew Lukas was home. He bounded across the deck and into the living room, dropping his helmet, skateboard, and backpack onto the floor. Even after all these months living with the neatest man on the planet, Lukas still had an unparalleled ability to turn any clean area into an instant mess. Pig-Pen would be proud of him. The Chalamet hair was soaked with sweat and there was an additional streak of wetness down his back. Seeing us staring at him, Lukas pulled his arm across his forehead in a desperate attempt to dry off.

"How was your last day of work?" my dad asked, trying to avoid the more substantial question at hand.

"It was awesome. I mean, I'll miss working with the kids," Lukas replied. He had changed a lot over the past few months.

"And where have you been since camp ended?" I added. I had a feeling I knew where he was and who he was with—and why.

"Always checking in on me," Lukas laughed. "I was at the Top of Topanga with Emery. We were talking about... what happens next."

"You heard from your dad, then?" I asked. Lukas confirmed he had gotten a voicemail. "Did you call your dad back?" I asked.

"No," Lukas said, getting quiet. "I wanted to see you before I called him back."

"Do you want to talk about it? Do you need help making a decision?" I offered. I wanted Lukas to know he was supported. I knew he valued my opinion.

"No. I just wanted to see you," he said. He seemed overly stoic.

I grew nervous. "I know," I replied. "What are you going to do?"

"Call him back," Lukas replied matter-of-factly. "I know what to do."

Lukas pulled his phone out of his pocket and headed out to the deck, sliding the door shut behind him. I was tempted to try to listen, but I wanted to give him his privacy.

The conversation became heated very quickly. I saw Lukas gesticulating wildly. After a few minutes of this, he slammed his hand down onto the deck railing, and quickly disconnected. He then slumped over for a moment, alone. I had a feeling it didn't go well.

"Don't say anything when he gets back in," my dad suggested, watching. Lukas stayed bent over the railing for what seemed to be an eternity.

I started fidgeting in my seat as we waited. "Should I go out there?" I asked.

"Be patient," Dad said. I leaned over on the sofa to get a better look, and hit the remote control by accident. Another episode of *Silver Spoons* appeared on the screen. It looked to be the pilot.

Ricky: Pleased to meet'cha. I'm your son.

Edward: Son? SON? Gee, I... yeah, but, but, but. When? Who?

The laugh track went crazy. If only life had such an easily-accessible laugh track.

The episode kept playing as Lukas finally came in from the deck. He plopped down on the sofa next to me, kicked off his black Converse high tops and looked at the TV.

"Awesome, dude, *Silver Spoons*. My favorite." He asked me to turn up the sound.

I looked at my dad and then at Lukas. I turned up the sound.

"Well?" I asked.

"Well, what's for dinner?" He rubbed his stomach.

"That's it?" I replied. Lukas was just watching *Silver Spoons*. He mouthed the dialogue whenever Edward and Ricky spoke. Apparently, he didn't know Kate's lines.

"Yeah, what's for dinner?" he said finally. "I'm famished."

My dad starting laughing. "Nothing's for dinner, unless you come clean," he said.

"About?" Lukas remained focused on the TV.

"The phone call." I pointed to the cell phone in his hand.

"Oh, that. Can you wait until *Silver Spoons* is over? I like this episode." Lukas seemed to be playing the avoidance game.

I grabbed the remote and turned off the TV. "There, it's over."

Lukas turned and faced me at last. "So, yeah," he said, a little shyly for him. "I told my dad I'm staying."

Dad applauded. I let out a huge sigh of relief.

Lukas smiled. "Topanga Canyon is my home now."

CREDITS

Topanga Sign Photo, © 2018. Eric A. Walters.

Additional Credits

Handprint Photos, © Shutterstock.

Royalty-free stock photo ID 1390098083 with Shutterstock Enhanced License.

British Soap Opera Dialogue, © 2019. ITV.

iCarly Theme, "Leave It All to Me." © 2007. Michael Corcoran and Dan Schneider.

Silver Spoons Theme, "Together." © 1982. Rik Howard and Bob Worth.

Unter Uns Theme, "Under One Roof." © 1995.

B.O.S., Ariola Records.

Topanga Map Designs by Imesami (fiverr.com)

Book Design by weformat (fiverr.com)

Book Cover Design by weformat (fiverr.com)

ABOUT THE AUTHOR

Eric Walters was born and raised in Massachusetts. He is a nationally-recognized science and technology educator and has authored several books and articled on innovative teaching and learning. He currently lives in New York City and has a deep affinity for Southern California, especially In N Out Burger and Paramount Studios. *My Life With Lukas (On Topanga Canyon Boulevard): Tailspin* is his third publication.

My Life With Lukas (On Topanga Canyon Boulevard): The Photos was published in summer 2018; *My Life With Lukas (On Topanga Canyon Boulevard): Junior Year* was published in winter 2018. *My Life With Lukas (On Topanga Canyon Boulevard): Best Kid Ever* was published in fall 2019.

www.ingramcontent.com/pod-product-compliance
Lightning Source LLC
Chambersburg PA
CBHW071558110726
47908CB00007B/2156